JASON AND THE ARGONAUTS

Retold by Felicity Brooks

Illustrated by Graham Humphreys

Designed by Kathy Ward

Edited by Jenny Tyler

CONTENTS

Chapter one

THE WICKED STEPMOTHER

Princess Helle and Prince Phrixus lived in a white marble palace. They had beautiful clothes, lots of toys and plenty of friends. At the snap of their fingers slaves would come running to bring them anything they wanted – a bowl of juicy fresh figs, a slice of bread and honey, or their own little chariot drawn by two donkeys.

They should have been the happiest children in Greece.

But since their stepmother Ino had arrived at the palace, everything had changed. All Ino ever did was complain. She walked around the palace with her two sons, inspecting things, moving things and shrieking if she found anything not to her liking. And Helle and Phrixus were never to Ino's liking. In short, they could do nothing right.

Try as they might to avoid her, by hiding behind the tall white columns in the courtyard or rushing into the garden at the sound of her approach, whenever their stepmother finally caught up with them they always seemed to be

doing something wrong. And on this particular day, when Ino had found them frantically trying to piece together a broken jar which had somehow fallen from the table, and was yelling at Helle and telling her what a wicked and ungrateful girl she was, Phrixus had caught his little sister's eye and

they'd both started to giggle.

Then Ino screamed even louder so all the dogs started barking and the slaves came running and Ino had exploded: "GET THESE VILE LITTLE MONSTERS OUT OF MY SIGHT THIS INSTANT!"

Phrixus and Helle hated her.

Now the unhappy prince was sitting upstairs on his bed with his hands clamped over his ears and his eyes shut tight, trying very hard to erase the image of his stepmother's hate-filled face from his mind. But nothing could drown out the voice from the room below and the bitter words which hammered through the ceiling and ricocheted around the room.

"You let them get away with murder, Athamas," Ino was shouting at Phrixus's father, "while my darling boys get nothing."

The king's quiet reply didn't penetrate as far as the bedroom, but Phrixus could imagine his father's swift denials. He knew that Athamas did his best to treat all the children equally, but Ino was convinced otherwise.

"Just because Nephele couldn't maintain discipline in this house, does not mean that *I* will allow your children to run riot," screeched the voice.

Phrixus screwed up his eyes and tried to think about his real mother, Nephele, the beautiful cloud spirit. He'd nearly managed to picture her smiling mouth and sparkling eyes, when the voice blotted everything out again.

"The country is going to rack and ruin, the people are starving and it's all *their* fault." Ino yelled.

Down in the room below, King Athamas sat stupefied, staring at his new wife in silence as she continued her hysterical tirade. It was hard to believe that this was the same woman he had married – the woman he had left Nephele for. Before she had seemed so gentle, so sweet. Now she was like a different person – always yelling and shrieking, ranting and raving and waving her arms around.

"Ask the oracle, then you'll see," she screamed, stabbing the air with a bony finger. "They've done this, your little monsters. The vile way they behave has angered the gods, and now we are paying for it."

It was true that all over the land the crops had failed. The fields had been tilled, the seeds planted and the soil watered as usual, but nothing had come of it. Not a single seed had sprouted. Winter was approaching and the granaries were nearly empty. For the first time in living memory, the people of Orchomenos, the city in the Kingdom of Boeotia where Phrixus and Helle lived, faced famine.

They had made sacrifices to Demeter, the goddess of the fruitful earth, hoping that she would take pity on them and make the corn grow.

They'd called upon all-powerful Zeus to help them and made offerings to great Hera the queen of the gods, but nothing worked.

Little did they know that the failure of the crops was no punishment from the gods, but the result of a malevolent and deliberate human act. It was the work of Ino herself.

So convinced was the new queen that Athamas treated Phrixus and Helle better than her own sons, that, driven by jealousy, she had devised a plot to get rid of them. The previous spring she had ordered her maids to sneak into the granaries at night and light fires under the corn seed, knowing full well that the smoke would spoil the seeds, so none would sprout.

And now her plan was working. King Athamas would do anything to prevent his people from suffering. He needed to know why the crops had failed and what could be done about it, and the only way to find out was to ask the oracle at Delphi, where a priestess would supply an answer from Mother Earth herself.

"We will consult the oracle," said Athamas calmly. "Please arrange it."

So messengers were dispatched to Delphi that very same day, and everyone waited anxiously for their return. When they finally arrived back at the palace, no one knew that Ino had already intercepted them outside the city gates and paid them to tell the king a monstrous and dreadful lie:

"You must sacrifice your children to Zeus," declared one of the messengers the minute Athamas stepped into the room. "That is what the oracle said. It's the only way to appease the gods and avert the famine." Athamas stood rooted to the spot in shock as the messenger parroted the cruel words that Ino had taught him.

"Take them to Mount Laphystium and kill them," said the other, thrusting a gleaming hunting knife into the king's trembling hand.

"When Zeus receives his sacrifice, the corn will grow."

Zeus was king of the gods and father of the human race. He could summon a storm in an instant, destroy whole cities with one strike of his thunderbolt, or set the earth spinning out of control if he so desired. No one disobeyed him. Ever.

"If it is Zeus's wish, then it must be done," said Athamas finally in a flat and resolute voice. "Tell the children to be ready at dawn."

The next morning, just as the sun was rising, Athamas led Phrixus and Helle up Mount Laphystium. Slung over his shoulder was an enormous bow and a quiver of arrows. At his side hung the knife in a leather sheath. He'd told the children they were going hunting. Athamas hardly said a word as he trudged up the steep rocky path.

Helle darted to and fro behind him, picking wild flowers and chatting cheerfully to her brother. It was a relief to be away from the palace and the disapproving glares and shrill voice of their stepmother. Far away in the distance stretched a sparkling expanse of water, and high overhead three huge black vultures soared on ragged wings. The air smelled sweet and clean.

Athamas stopped to catch his breath, leaning heavily against a rocky outcrop. A lizard darted into a crevice. The king bent down to remove a stone from his sandal, then brought his gaze back to rest on the children, watching in silence as Phrixus chased Helle between the rocks. Helle was squealing in excitement.

How could he bring himself to perform the terrible act that Zeus demanded? How could Zeus demand such a terrible act? Athamas wrapped his hand around the sturdy handle of the hunting knife. Which of his children should he sacrifice first? Should he force Helle to watch her own father kill her brother? Or let Phrixus see him slash his sister's throat? Little Helle was always so trusting. Athamas started to imagine what would happen to her sparkling eyes if. . . but that would be nothing compared to the pain, fear and incomprehension that would cloud her features when she realized the knife was also meant for her. . .

"When Zeus receives his sacrifice,

the corn will grow." Those had been the messenger's words. Thousands of people were relying on Athamas to do something. What could be worse: the sacrifice of his children or the harrowing scenes he knew he must witness if he let his kingdom starve?

He turned away from the children and looked out across the rivers and valleys of Boeotia to the sunlit plain beyond. The sky was clear except for one wispy cloud drifting slowly across the mountain top. The meadows below should have been filled with the swaying heads of ripe, golden corn ready for reaping, but every field as far as the eye could see was barren, brown and bare.

"Zeus must be obeyed," said Athamas under his breath, steeling himself for the gruesome task ahead. Helle was now sitting on a rock at the side of the path, singing a reaper's song as she knotted her flowers into a garland.

He would kill her first, Athamas decided. Then he wouldn't have to see her face when he took the knife to Phrixus. . .

He began collecting rocks to build an altar. It was usually the job of the priests to make sacrifices, but he would just have to do his best.

Helle placed her garland around her neck, jumped to her feet and came skipping down the path, curious to find out what her father was doing. Her brother was nowhere to be seen.

"In the name of Zeus, the great father of our race, the mighty and all powerful, this sacrifice will be made," muttered Athamas, hoping that if he kept the sacrificial incantations quiet enough, Helle would not be alarmed before it was absolutely necessary.

❧━◆⬦◆⬦◆⬦◆⬦◆⬦◆⬦◆━❧

Helle may not have heard her father's chanting, but far away on Mount Olympus, the home of the gods, someone else's ears pricked up. The king of the gods could hear a feather fall in a distant forest or a lobster walking on the seabed, and now, above the morning cacophony of singing birds, bleating goats, barking dogs and petals dropping from flowers all over Boeotia, he heard someone whisper his name.

He looked across to Mount Laphystium. Near the peak, a boy was playing. Farther down, a little girl was skipping along a path, calling to a man who was constructing a sacrificial altar. . . and carrying a large knife.

Zeus sighed. *People!* He really despaired of them sometimes. Surely they knew he hated human sacrifice – and this was being done in his name! Something had to be done.

Zeus summoned Hermes, his son and messenger, and at that same moment Hera, his wife, and Nephele, Helle's mother, arrived, breathless and agitated.

"Have you seen what's going on over there?" said Hera, pointing in the direction of Mount Laphystium.

"Indeed," said Zeus.

"Nephele just told me," continued Hera. "She was floating over the mountain, keeping an eye on her children, when she realized what Athamas was up to. Something must be done to stop it."

Hera put a protective arm around Nephele's shoulder to try to comfort her. Zeus turned to his son.

"Fetch the golden ram from Mycenae," he said. "And hurry."

Hermes clicked his winged sandals together, flew up into the air, and then shot off over the mountain top in the direction of Mycenae.

Back on Mount Laphystium, Athamas was finishing his preparations. He poured wine from a flask over the altar then gently lifted Helle up onto it and instructed her to lie down. The little girl was happy to join in with his game and Athamas was relieved that she seemed to have no idea what was going on. Gulping back his tears, he stretched his hands up to the heavens and called upon Zeus.

When he'd finished this final chant, he reached down to draw the knife, grasped its handle firmly and raised the blade high into the air. Helle saw the knife flashing in the sunlight and screamed. At the same instant Phrixus came racing down the path. He was momentarily dazzled by the sun glinting off the blade, but then recoiled in horror as he realized what was about to happen.

"No!" he gasped.

The blade hovered in midair as Athamas was temporarily distracted by his son's cry.

"Zeus must be obeyed," hissed the king through gritted teeth, tears now pouring down his face. Helle lay paralyzed with shock staring up at the knife point directly above her.

Suddenly the scene was thrown into shadow as a large shape loomed overhead. Phrixus looked up. Floating just above Helle, its fleece sparkling in the sunlight, was an enormous golden ram!

"Climb onto my back!" urged a voice.

Helle lifted herself onto her feet, grabbed the ram's thick, woolly fleece and climbed onto its back.

"Take me too!" pleaded Phrixus, throwing himself at the ram and hauling himself up.

"Hold on tight!" said the voice. It belonged to Hermes, who was floating, invisible, at the ram's side.

Athamas looked on in disbelief as the ram flew over his head and disappeared into the distance over the top of the mountain.

Phrixus and Helle clung tightly to the ram as it whisked them away, higher and higher into the clear, blue sky. Both still too shocked to say anything, they watched in silence as

"Take me too!" pleaded Phrixus

they passed over a narrow piece of land and then out over the huge expanse of the Aegean Sea. Far, far below were scattered islands of all shapes and sizes, like jigsaw puzzle pieces thrown from a box.

"Where are we going?" Phrixus asked finally, but the ram had no voice of its own, and Hermes was already on his way back home.

Now that they were out of danger, Helle was beginning to recover. In fact she had started to enjoy herself. It was fun flying fast on the back of a soft golden ram with the warm autumn wind in her hair. Sometimes they flew through a cloud or surprised a flock of birds. Once they came across a group of storks flapping their stately way across the sea.

"Look!" called Phrixus. He was pointing down to a narrow strip of sea between two headlands. The ram seemed to be flying straight down to it, shooting through the air like an arrow.

"Faster!" cried Helle, clapping her hands in delight. It was then that it happened. Helle fell. And before Phrixus could grab her, she was plummeting through the air with a terrified scream, her long, dark hair streaming out behind her as she tumbled wildly down toward the sea. Down to her watery death.

To this day, the spot where the little princess drowned is known as the Hellespont, which means "Helle's Sea",

in her memory.

Phrixus clung on grimly for the rest of the journey, scarcely able to take in what had happened. He was suddenly very frightened. He was hundreds of miles from home, now high above the Black Sea, and the ram showed no sign of slowing down or landing. His sister was missing – probably dead – and he had no idea where he was going or what lay in store for him when he arrived. And it was getting dark.

When the ram finally came to land, Phrixus found himself in the grounds of a royal palace in a kingdom called Colchis which was ruled by King Aites. The king seemed overjoyed that Phrixus had arrived on the back of the golden ram and welcomed him. The ram was – he explained to Phrixus – a symbol of sovereignty. It had been sent by to Colchis by the gods as a sign to show that he – Aites – was the rightful king of that land.

There remained only one thing to do, said King Aites – sacrifice the ram to Zeus and dedicate its fleece to him. This would be a way of giving thanks for Phrixus's escape and ensure the great god always looked down kindly on the kingdom.

The ceremony was performed the very next day and the fleece was hung in an oak tree in the sacred Grove of Ares where it was guarded night and day by a huge dragon.

The story of Helle and Phrixus

and the golden ram spread far and wide and soon everyone knew about the golden fleece hanging in an oak tree near the palace in Colchis.

But what became of Ino, the wicked stepmother, and the people of Boeotia? When the messengers heard about the children's miraculous escape, one of them blurted out that Ino had bribed them to tell a lie about what the oracle had said. Then Ino's maids confessed that she had made them spoil the corn seed, so her whole evil plot was uncovered.

Ino fled from the palace and ran to a cliff where she hurled herself into the sea and was drowned. Hera and Nephele did their utmost to persuade Zeus that Athamas should die too, but the king of the gods did not believe he deserved such a harsh punishment. Instead, Athamas was banished from Boeotia and spent years wandering in the wilderness before he met his third wife and raised a new family.

The people of Boeotia just survived the winter and Demeter ensured that they had a plentiful and early harvest the following year.

And as for Phrixus, he stayed in Colchis and when he grew up, married one of King Aites's daughters, named Chalciope. He often passed the Grove of Ares and when he saw the huge hissing dragon and the Golden Fleece sparkling in the sunshine, he was reminded of the day on the mountain when he and his sister were rescued by the ram, and he thought about little Helle and the terrible moment when she had plunged to her death in the sea.

It was many years later that Jason, a young prince from Thessaly in Greece, set out to bring the Golden Fleece back to his homeland. But that's the next story.

Chapter two

JASON'S JOURNEY

Jason was sitting close to the fire inside the mountain cave that was his home. It was a very special day. The sun had risen over Mount Pelion, just as it always did and Jason had spent the morning doing archery and athletics, just as he always did. But this was the day he had been waiting for, the day he would finally find out the truth. Chiron had promised.

Chiron was a centaur – half man and half horse – and the only father Jason had ever known. For eighteen years the huge, kindly creature had looked after him and taught him about music and medicine, hunting and fighting. Jason now knew the names of all the mountain herbs and which ailments they could cure. He could kill a wild deer with one throw of a javelin or spear, draw a full-sized bow, recite poetry, tell stories of great heroes, and play the lyre so melodiously that even the rabbits stopped in their tracks and pricked up their ears to listen.

But he had absolutely no idea who he was.

A long time ago he had realized that the centaur was not his real father.

A little later he began to wonder why he didn't have a mother. But whenever he asked Chiron where his real parents were, and why he lived in a cave, when, if he stood on a rocky outcrop and looked down to the valley below, he could see villages and farms and even a city clinging to the coast at the edge of a shimmering sea, the wise old centaur sighed deeply, fixed his eyes on the distant horizon and said simply:

"When you are older, Jason. Then you shall know."

And at last that day had come. Chiron had promised to tell Jason everything, and now he sat on the other side of the fire, staring into the flames and occasionally poking the logs with the tip of his long wooden staff. His face was bathed in a warm golden glow, and the smoke which curled over his beard and up into the roof of the cave made his eyes water slightly.

The crackling of the fire was accompanied by the dripping of water at the cave mouth. Outside it was pouring with rain.

"Your father is called Aeson," said Chiron suddenly, "the rightful king of Iolcus. Your real name is Diomedes."

Jason felt a little shiver run down his spine. He sat bolt upright and listened carefully.

"You were born in Thessaly, in the royal palace at Iolcus – the city on the coast – you can see it from here on a clear day. Your mother is called Polymele."

Chiron paused to clear his throat and add another log to the fire. The rain beat down hard on the compacted red earth at the cave mouth, sending snake-like trickles in toward the fire. The centaur shifted into a more comfortable position, settling on his haunches to continue the story.

"From the moment you were born, you were in terrible danger – in such great danger, in fact, that your mother pretended you had been born dead and smuggled you out of the palace to me. Keeping you away from human eyes was your only chance of survival, because your father's throne had just been seized by his half-brother, Pelias." Chiron spat out the name as though it were a piece of rancid meat.

"You and your father are descendants of Aeolus," Chiron continued. "And Pelias had been told by the oracle that he would be killed by an Aeolian. So he imprisoned your father in the deepest dungeon of Iolcus and swore to kill all his children. Fortunately your mother's plan worked and you came safely to me."

Jason wrinkled his brow in concentration. There was so much to take in.

"So where is he now, my father?" he asked finally.

"Still in prison, as far as I know," replied Chiron.

"And my mother?"

"Still at the palace."

"And Pelias?"

"Still in power."

"So what should I do?" asked Jason eagerly. Suddenly incensed, he jumped to his feet and grabbed a spear.

"Nothing at this time of night," said Chiron calmly, "but at sunrise tomorrow you should leave for Iolcus. I have taught you all I know and you are ready to make your own way in the world."

Chiron was still staring at the dancing flames, but his eyes had begun to glaze over as they always did when he was about to see into the future. He started to rock back and forth on his huge haunches, humming softly to himself. Then he spoke slowly in a halting, growling voice.

"I see fame and glory. . . and a long, long journey. I see pain. . . and tragedy. . . and a chance to wear a crown."

Jason begged him to explain, but Chiron was already out of his trance and poking at the glowing embers of the fire with his stick. The twinkle had returned to his eyes and the gnarled old face had regained its serene expression. He would say no more.

The next morning at first light, Jason was preparing himself for his journey to Iolcus. He put on a leather tunic, wrapped a leopard skin around his shoulders, strapped on his sandals and armed himself with two spears and a wooden staff. When he had eaten the bread and honey that Chiron provided and listened to his directions for Iolcus, he said a sad goodbye to the centaur and set off down the steep winding path that led to the valley below.

Chiron smiled to himself as the handsome young man disappeared from view. He'd seen many other young warriors set off down the same path – Achilles, Castor and Polydeuces had all left their childhood home as bright-eyed and eager young men and were now celebrated in poems and stories as great heroes. The centaur felt sure the same fate lay in store for Jason.

It was a fine spring morning. The sky was clear, but the ground was still very wet. Jason whistled loudly and thwacked at the damp undergrowth with his staff, sending flurries of small chattering birds up into the air. Soon he emerged from the trees into a meadow where a carpet of yellow flowers spread out before him. *King's Spears* was what Chiron called them. Crickets jumped and chirped, larks sang high above, and somewhere down below came the sound of bells as a goatherd drove his flock to new pastures.

Jason walked all morning. When

. . . and set off down the steep winding path

he reached the pine-scented foothills, the path evened out and by lunchtime he was down in the valley heading for Iolcus. The sun had dried the last of the puddles, so the going was easy. As he marched along, Jason gradually became aware of a dull roaring sound in the distance.

When he had walked a little farther, a river came into view, but it was not the sluggish, meandering stream Chiron had described, but a seething, thunderous torrent. The downpour of the night before and the thawing snows from Mount Pelion had swelled the River Anaurus to an angry swirling mass.

The path to Iolcus continued on the other bank, but if there ever had been a bridge spanning the water, there was absolutely no sign of it now.

Jason sat down on the bank and took a lump of bread from his bag. He was just chewing the last mouthful, staring at the muddy water and wondering how he could cross, when he felt a tap on his shoulder. Jumping in surprise, he twisted his head around to see an old woman standing behind him. She was dressed in rags and bent nearly double over a walking stick. He had no idea where she'd come from.

"Young man," she croaked, "please be so kind as to help me cross the river."

Jason gulped down the bread and did his best to sound polite.

"If you want to risk a ride on my back, you are more than welcome," he said "but I was just wondering how I was going to manage it myself. It could be dangerous."

"I'll take that chance," said the old lady. "You won't regret it," she added.

He strapped his weapons and bag to his side and carefully lifted the frail old woman onto his back. She clung to his neck with her bony fingers as he grabbed an overhanging branch and slowly lowered himself into the river. It was icy cold.

He took a cautious step forward, then planted his foot firmly and let go of the branch. The rushing water surged all around them. The current was stronger than he had feared and with each new step he struggled harder to keep his foothold on the slippery rocks of the riverbed.

When he'd first hoisted the old lady onto his back, she'd felt as light as a sparrow, but the farther and deeper they went, the heavier she seemed to get, until he felt as though he was carrying a huge lead weight on his back. He knew that if he put one foot wrong, they would both be swept downstream and dashed on the rocks below.

In the middle of the river, Jason eased his foot forward and was momentarily almost completely submerged. When his next staggering

step raised his face back above the surface, he spluttered and gasped for air. Roaring icy water filled his ears and stung his eyes, but somehow he managed to keep hold of his heavy passenger as he inched, step by careful step, across to the opposite bank. Finally he made a grab for a tree root and hauled himself up onto the grass. He set the old lady down gently before throwing himself to the ground where he lay panting with exhaustion and rubbing his eyes.

"Well, I don't want to do that again in a hurry!" he said, when he had recovered enough breath to speak. There was no answer.

He sat up and turned to face the old woman, but she had disappeared! Jason was mystified.

Back up on Mount Olympus, the home of the gods, Hera looked down kindly on the bedraggled young man, as he picked pieces of weed from his tunic and wrung the water from his sodden clothes. He did not know that the frail old woman he had just carried so courageously across the river had been the great goddess Hera herself, in disguise.

Hera had heard that over in Iolcus, King Pelias was about to celebrate a festival to Poseidon, the sea god, but he had forgotten about her. This had infuriated her, so she decided to find a mortal who would side with her against Pelias, and this young man had just passed her test.

If, when she was disguised, he had refused to help her cross the river, or dropped her in midstream when she pushed down on his back with the weight of two centaurs, she would now be cursing him. Instead she was ready to reward him and help him on his way.

Jason had no idea that Hera was watching him as he got back onto his feet. Unable to explain the old woman's sudden disappearance, he decided to concentrate on the task in hand – the completion of his journey. Only now did he realize that during the crossing he had somehow lost one of his sandals. He threw a quick glance down the river to see if it had become lodged between the rocks farther downstream, but there was no sign of it. Undaunted, he gathered up his things and set off.

The rest of the journey was fairly uneventful. The soles of his feet had been toughened by his rugged mountain existence, so he was not too worried by the absence of one sandal. The warm afternoon sun soon dried his damp clothes, and the soggy remains of the bread in his bag, along with a few wild berries, just about took the edge off his hunger that evening.

When he was too weary to walk a step farther and just as the sun was setting, he found an abandoned shepherd's hut where the hooting of owls and the bleating of lambs lulled him quickly to sleep.

By mid-morning the next day, Jason was wandering through the marketplace of Iolcus, gaping at the enormous buildings and the hundreds of people with their babbling voices that filled the square.

The handsome young stranger with his long yellow hair certainly attracted plenty of attention. Everywhere he went, people would look at him, then turn away and whisper to each other behind their hands. His clothes were not very different from those of several others in the crowd, although perhaps a little scruffier, and he was sure he hadn't suddenly sprouted an extra head, so he really couldn't understand what it was that was arousing such curiosity.

He decided to find out.

Stopping at a fish stall, he asked the stallholder what was causing the stir.

"Your feet, sir," replied the man.

"My feet?" said Jason.

"Well, not exactly your feet, but your sandals – or rather your sandal. It's the oracle, you see, sir. The oracle told King Pelias that one day he would lose his kingdom to a *monosandalos* – a man wearing only one sandal."

"Well, that explains it," said Jason, rather relieved. He thanked the man and strode on to the palace.

News of the stranger with one sandal had reached the king ahead of Jason himself, so Pelias was not at all surprised when a young man arrived demanding to see him.

"So, *boy*, you have come to claim my kingdom, have you?" sneered Pelias when Jason had explained why he had come.

"My father's kingdom," Jason corrected him.

"Your father is dead," Pelias lied, "but if you really think you are worthy to wear the crown of Iolcus, then you must prove it."

Pelias was playing for time. The people were obviously impressed by this confident young man, and many remembered his father, King Aeson, and the way he had been treated. Pelias couldn't just cart the interloper off to the dungeon as he would have wished, or he might have a riot on his hands. His spies in the marketplace had made that quite clear. Instead he needed to find another way to get rid of him.

"Bring me the Golden Fleece from Colchis," said Pelias, "then Iolcus shall be yours."

Pelias well knew that the voyage to Colchis would be long and dangerous, that King Aites would fight to the death rather than lose the fleece, and that it was guarded night and day by a huge, fire-breathing dragon. He confidently expected that Jason would refuse to accept the challenge, or that if he did accept it, he would never return.

Jason looked around the hall. All eyes seemed to be on him and there was an expectant hush. He knew about the Golden Fleece and the story of Phrixus and Helle from tales Chiron had told around the fire on winter evenings. He thought about the wise old centaur's words the night before he left: *"fame and glory. . . a long, long journey. . . a chance to wear a crown."*

This was what he'd come for. This was his chance. The quest would be perilous, of that he could be sure, but there was no turning back now.

Jason drew himself up to his full height and looked Pelias squarely in the eye.

"Yes, I'll bring you the Golden Fleece," he said.

Chapter three

THE QUEST BEGINS

"CREW MEMBERS NEEDED! CREW MEMBERS NEEDED! Listen, good citizens and listen well! Jason, a Prince from Thessaly, is going on an expedition across the Black Sea to get the Golden Fleece and is looking for crew members. Only the fearless need apply. . ."

The market squares of every city in Greece were soon echoing to the cries of messengers as they made this announcement.

It hadn't taken Jason long to realize that the quest for the Golden Fleece would be much too difficult and dangerous to attempt alone. Colchis was a long way from Iolcus, across a stretch of ocean ruled by an extremely irritable sea god and fabled to be full of monsters, whirlpools and other unknown perils. He needed a sturdy ship and courageous crew to stand a chance of getting there in one piece.

The news spread fast and people came flocking – great Greek heroes, experienced rowers and celebrated athletes, as well as any number of unknown but eager young men. It was a hard job to choose between them.

Even Heracles turned up. This was not just any old Greek hero but *the* Heracles, the famous, incredibly brave, son of Zeus, lover of danger and strongest man in the world volunteering to join the crew! Jason was astounded. But the surprises did not stop there.

Atalanta arrived. She was the best archer in the land and also a brilliant runner and survival expert, and with her came Zetes and Calais, the winged sons of Boreas, the North Wind, who, like their father, could fly through the air faster than an arrow.

Next came the twins, Castor and Polydeuces, one a wrestler and the other a boxer and both Olympic champions. A man called Nauplius was chosen as navigator, Tiphys as helmsman and Lynceus as lookout. His eyesight was so sharp he could spot an ant from miles away. Echion, the son of Hermes, was chosen as messenger and herald, and Orpheus, a famous poet and musician, offered to provide entertainment on the long journey. The music of his magical lyre was so enchanting, it could even soothe savage monsters, people said.

And there were many others, all chosen for their remarkable talents and all eager for excitement and danger. Some could understand the language of animals or see into the future. There was a man who was indestructible in battle, another who could sprint over water, and a shape-shifter named Periclymenus who could turn himself into anything he wanted to be.

Altogether fifty-three were selected. Even King Pelias's own son, Acastus, was taken on. Pelias was reluctant to let

him go at first, but soon realized that if he made too much fuss, it would become obvious that he thought the whole expedition was doomed, so Acastus joined the quest.

While Jason was busy choosing the crew, a craftsman called Argus was standing on the seashore up to his knees in sawdust. He had been put in charge of building the ship, but he was not alone in his task.

Great Athene herself, daughter of Zeus and goddess of wisdom and war, went to Mount Pelion to cut down the trees for the timber. She chose the tallest, straightest spruce she could find for the mast, then instructed Argus how to prepare the wood and build the ship. She made sure that the hull was watertight, that the huge sail was woven from the strongest linen and that every one of the fifty oars was planed to perfection.

As a special gift to Jason, she fitted a piece of carved wood into the front of the ship, at the prow. This wood came from her father's sacred oak tree at Dodona and it gave the prow a magical ability – it could speak in a human voice.

When the ship was finished, Athene named it the *Argo*, then, hitching a ride on a cloud, she disappeared back to Mount Olympus before the crew came down to the beach to inspect Argus's handiwork.

With cries of "Wonderful!" and "Well done Argus!" they climbed up onto the deck and found their places on the rowing benches where they ran their hands appreciatively over the smoothly sanded oars, and admired the mast and sail.

"It was Athene's work," said Argus modestly, lapping up the praise.

Jason went to the prow to address them.

"Welcome," he shouted above the babble of excited voices. "Welcome on board the *Argo*."

The noise died down and everyone turned to face him.

"Thank you all," he continued, "for volunteering to join the quest for the Golden Fleece. From this day on you shall be known as 'The Argonauts', and I hope you are all prepared for adventure. . . and some strenuous rowing!"

A ripple of laughter swept through the crew.

"Nobody knows what dangers lie ahead," said Jason more solemnly. "And anyone who does not feel confident that they really want to be part of this expedition must say so now. It will be your last chance."

He paused and surveyed the crowd of faces, waiting for a voice to break the silence. None came.

"In the morning," he resumed, "if the wind is in the right direction, we'll be on our way, but first—"

He stepped down onto the deck and made his way to an empty bench.

"—we need to choose a captain."

There was a moment's surprised hush, then some hesitant whispering, before some of the younger men turned to Heracles, automatically expecting that the famous warrior would volunteer. But the big man remained seated and raised his hand to quieten their shouts of encouragement.

"I wouldn't accept the job, even

if it were offered," he said resolutely. "There's only one person here who should lead us – and that's the man who accepted this challenge in the first place. That man is Jason."

There was some muted muttering, followed by the beginnings of a round of applause which built to a crescendo when Jason made his way back to the prow to take command, grinning from ear to ear.

~❖~

"Well I'm glad that's decided," said Hera to Athene, up on Mount Olympus. "I never could stand that Heracles – all brawn and no brain he is – the result of one of your father's. . . How can I put this? Let's just say one of your father's little liaisons with a mortal. If they'd chosen *him* as captain, I'd have gone out of my way to make trouble."

"Well, it's a good thing they didn't then," said Athene with heartfelt relief.

She had seen her stepmother "make trouble" before.

"But *he's* going to be a splendid leader!" said Hera tenderly, looking down on Jason who was heaving a large wooden chest up onto the *Argo*. "And about time too! It's been ages since I had a real hero to take care of – not since the Trojan War in fact. I'm really looking forward to this!"

"So am I," said Athene quietly. "So am I."

~❖~

The *Argo*'s captain worked harder than anyone that afternoon when they were hauling all the equipment on board and dragging the ship down to the sea to launch her. At sunset, after they had made offerings to the god Apollo for a safe voyage, they held a feast on the shore. Orpheus played and sang while the glow from an immense fire lit up the Argonauts' happy faces.

Unaware that he was being watched by Hera and Athene, Jason sat back and surveyed the scene. It would be hard to fail with such a wonderful ship and crew, he told himself. Even so, he offered his own quiet prayer to the gods, just in case.

The celebration went on well into the night until eventually everyone fell asleep on the beach under a clear sky studded with stars.

"Argonauts! Argonauts!
Morning has come,
The wind is set fair,
And there's work to be done.

Argonauts! Argonauts!
Time to away,
Your vessel is waiting,
You must not delay."

It was the voice of the magic prow calling them on board that roused the crew the next morning. The rosy pink glow of dawn was spreading across the sky, and a small group of well-wishers had gathered on the beach to wave them off.

Among them were Chiron, the centaur, and Jason's mother, Polymele. She had only just been reunited with her son, but if she was at all anxious about his safety, her face showed only pride as she watched the ship cutting swiftly through the silvery morning mist out of the bay and disappearing from view into the open sea.

As soon as the *Argo* had cleared the bay, the sail was raised and a stiff breeze drove the ship forward. The rowers could relax. Jason stood at the prow, watching dolphins leaping and chattering in their strange, clicking tongue.

"They're wishing us luck," shouted Melampus, who could understand animals.

For four days they rowed and sailed across the Aegean, stopping each night on an island, or coming into the coast to rest. On the evening of the fifth day, the wind dropped just as the sun was setting, but a short burst of energetic rowing brought them to the rocky island of Lemnos where they intended to stay the night.

Lynceus, the lookout, scanned the shore.

"Armed warriors on the beach!" he called.

When they drew closer everyone could see the group of islanders he had spotted. The last rays of the setting

The glow from an immense fire lit up the Argonauts' happy faces

sun glinted on the bronze helmets that covered their faces and they were brandishing their swords and spears menacingly.

"A fight – brilliant!" shouted Heracles, dropping his oar and grabbing his weapons. Atalanta seized her bow and sprang forward, but Jason motioned to them to sit back down and told Echion,

in around the bow.

"We come in peace," shouted Echion.

A murmur spread through the group.

"We're the Argonauts from Iolcus," he called. "We're sailing to the east to get the Golden Fleece. All we seek is shelter for the night – and perhaps some fresh water."

the herald, to come to the prow.

"Let's try talking first," said Jason. "We'll only resort to weapons if it looks like they're going to attack."

Heracles's face fell, but he and Atalanta did as they were told and went back to their places, grumbling discontentedly.

As Tiphys steered the *Argo* gently onto the beach, the islanders swarmed

There was no immediate response from the crowd below, but then the murmuring started again and grew louder, until one voice rang out above the others. It was higher than Echion had expected. It was the voice of a woman.

"We welcome you to Lemnos," said the voice. "Please come ashore."

The Argonauts disembarked and

the warriors took off their helmets to greet them. Their long, flowing locks were caught by the evening breeze. Not a single male face could be seen.

"I am Queen Hypsipyle," said the leader to Jason. "We don't usually greet strangers in such a hostile way, but we thought you were an enemy ship from Thrace."

"I see," said Jason.

The weary Argonauts needed little encouragement to accept the supper which the women offered to share with them. They greedily devoured large hunks of roast boar and washed it down with plenty of good Greek wine. Soon the night air was filled with the sound of laughter and music.

If Jason had known why there were no men on the island, he would certainly not have been so eager to share Queen Hypsipyle's supper, but only the gods and the women themselves were aware of a horrific event which the island had recently witnessed. There were no men on Lemnos because the women had killed them – every single one of them, except the queen's old father whose life she had secretly spared, setting him adrift in a boat.

It had all started when the women forgot to pay respect to Aphrodite, the goddess of beauty and love. As a punishment she afflicted them with a disgusting smell which their husbands found so revolting, they

sailed off to Thrace and brought back new partners. This, of course, had enraged their rejected wives who seized their husbands' weapons, drove the Thracian girls away, and turned on the men savagely, murdering all of them, including Hypsipyle's husband, the king.

And now they wanted some replacements. Since the foul smell had left them, the women of Lemnos had been looking for new husbands – and a new king. The extravagant show of friendship to which the Argonauts were treated over the next few days was designed to encourage them to stay for as long as possible – or hopefully forever.

After long hours of sitting on hard wooden rowing benches, heaving huge oars through choppy seas with blistered hands, most of the crew welcomed the hospitality and seemed reluctant to leave. And Jason was spending so much time with the queen, it was as if he'd forgotten all about his quest.

But by the fourth day, Heracles had become restless and irritable. He wandered down to the seashore with Atalanta where the deserted *Argo* sat on the sand, stranded by the low tide. They set up a lump of driftwood on a rock and began some archery practice.

"I came on this voyage for adventure and excitement," complained Heracles as they strode across the sand to retrieve their arrows, "Not a nonstop party with a bunch of islanders."

"Me too!" agreed Atalanta. "And there's something very odd about this place. I mean, where are all the men?"

"I asked one of the queen's servants about that," replied Heracles. "And do you know what she told me? She said that the women were treated so badly by their husbands, they grabbed all the men's weapons and drove them off the island."

"A likely story!" said Atalanta, screwing up one eye as she drew her bow. Her arrow shot through the air and thudded into the driftwood.

"So now they're looking for new ones, I suppose." Heracles said.

"New what?" asked Atalanta, preoccupied.

"Husbands!" laughed Heracles.

"Husbands," muttered Atalanta, reaching over her shoulder to pull another arrow from her quiver. "Husbands are nothing but trouble, may the gods save us from them!"

Another arrow hit its mark.

Even as they spoke, Jason was being made an offer it was very hard to refuse – the kingship of Lemnos. The vacant throne could be his, Queen Hypsipyle said, if the Argonauts stayed on the island and married the women. Jason was tempted. He even halfheartedly accepted, saying that as soon as he had completed the quest they would return.

But just at that moment Heracles and Atalanta came storming into the palace demanding that the Argonauts set sail immediately.

"We won't win any fame and glory here!" said Heracles, unable to conceal his frustration. "There's just nothing going on!"

Jason reluctantly agreed it was time to go. He said goodbye to the queen, solemnly promising he would return and marry her as soon as he could. He never did.

It was only much later, when they found out what had really taken place on Lemnos, that the Argonauts realized what a lucky escape they'd had. Who knows what might have happened if they had stayed? But for now, as they said their farewells on the shore, most were genuinely sad to leave.

Once out at sea, much to Atalanta and Heracles's relief, everyone soon stopped thinking about the women of Lemnos. A much greater challenge lay ahead – the navigation of the Hellespont.

This notoriously dangerous channel was the only way through to the east, but since the Trojan War, King Laomedon of Troy had barred it to Greek ships. They would have to try to slip through secretly at night, right under the noses of the Trojan soldiers who guarded its entrance. If they were caught, it would mean certain death.

As they were making their approach, a strong wind blew up from the south. All the lamps were extinguished and while the sail was being hoisted in the darkness, the rowers did their best to muffle their oars with strips of linen. The inky waters of the Hellespont swirled before them.

It was a cloudy, moonless night. Lynceus perched on the prow, peering through the gloom, but even his keen eyesight could scarcely make out the towering headlands at the channel's entrance. One false move could drive them onto the rocks or straight into the hands of their enemies.

At a signal from Jason, the sail was braced and the rowers heaved on their oars. The *Argo*, dwarfed by the cliffs on either side, cut rapidly through the churning water and into Trojan territory. The creaking of the mast sounded treacherously loud. The noise of each oar stroke seemed to echo for minutes.

No one dared say a word until they had left the Aegean far behind, and then they just whispered a prayer for their safe deliverance and steeled themselves to row through the night.

With the first glimmer of dawn, the Argonauts rowed out into the wide expanse of the Propontis, which today is known as the Sea of Marmara. They were safely through the Hellespont and, with a fair wind behind them, about to sail to the east, into the unknown.

Chapter four

ADVENTURES AND DANGERS

"Nothing but feasting and parties!" grumbled Heracles. "And not nearly enough action for my liking."

"So last night's adventure wasn't exciting enough?" said Tiphys, genuinely surprised.

"Oh, the great Heracles usually sails through enemy territory twice before breakfast!" mocked Atalanta playfully. "Nothing's exciting enough for him."

They were rowing the *Argo* around to the Dolionians' city port. The Dolionians lived on the rugged south shore of the Propontis, and when the weary Argonauts had arrived on their beach earlier that morning, their king, who was called Cyzicus, had come down to greet them. He was in the middle of celebrating his marriage, he told them proudly, to a beautiful princess called Cleite, and he would be delighted if they could all to come to his wedding feast.

"And why don't you bring your ship around to our port? It's just up the coast at the foot of Mount Dindymum. It will be safe there," he had added.

So this was what Atalanta, Heracles and Tiphys were now doing, while the other Argonauts were on their way to the wedding.

But Heracles was far from happy.

"I suppose it was a little scary, going through the Hellespont," he said, heaving on his oar in the shadow of the mighty mountain, "but what I want is some real advent— AAAH!" He had spoken too soon. For just at that instant an enormous wave hit him full in the face and flung him off the bench and onto the deck, where he lay winded and stunned.

Atalanta dropped her oar and looked up. A huge boulder was hurtling through the air in the direction of the ship! Before she had time to move, it had crashed into the water just inches from the prow and sent another massive wave smashing onto the *Argo*. The ship was tossed violently sideways, Atalanta was thrown to the deck, and when she came to her senses, found herself lying in a pool of water, half underneath a bench with her head close to Heracles's.

"What's happening?" he groaned,

raising his hand to a bleeding gash on his forehead.

"We're under attack!" said Atalanta, wiping the stinging salt water from her eyes. "From giants!"

Heracles lifted his head just in time to see a colossal figure snapping off the top of the mountain with one of its many hands and hurling it into the sea. Heracles gripped the bench tightly, shut his eyes and braced himself for the impact.

Another wall of water came pounding down. The *Argo* keeled over so far that Atalanta thought they would capsize.

"Is this dangerous enough for you?" she hissed through a veil of seaweed and straggling wet hair. "We're going to drown!"

Heracles ignored her, rubbed the water from his eyes and reached for his spear. Before the next wave could hit them, he had jumped to his feet and launched the weapon high into the air. It met its mark with a dull thud and a giant body came tumbling down the mountainside.

"One down!" cheered Atalanta, drawing her bow.

Her arrow flew through the air and hit its target between the eyes. The enormous, six-armed body toppled forward, rolled down the mountain and plunged headfirst into the sea.

"*Yes!*" called Tiphys from the helm, getting ready to shoot his own arrow.

The counter-attack seemed to have taken the giants by surprise. The hail of boulders suddenly stopped, and the remaining attackers just stood and stared, as though they couldn't quite believe what was happening. Their towering static forms made easy targets, and before long the last one was toppling face-first into the sea like a felled tree.

Atalanta and the others cheered, stowed away their weapons, rowed the *Argo* to the shore and waited for the return of their comrades.

The other Argonauts looked somewhat disappointed when they heard they had missed all the action, but not nearly as disappointed as Atalanta felt when they described the magnificent feast she had missed – whole roast deer, succulent wild boar, huge quantities of seafood and all the wine they could drink.

"Absolutely – HIC! – delicious," was Acastus's verdict.

King Cyzicus and some of the wedding party had come down to the port to see them off. The king, still wearing his wedding outfit – a lion skin draped over an ankle-length tunic – surveyed the enormous bodies that were lying face-down in the water, then turned to Jason.

"They usually left us in peace," he explained fretfully. "Poseidon saw to that – he was supposed to keep them under control, you see. But they

"We're under attack. . . From giants!"

always were frighteningly unpredictable – rather like their master," he added under his breath, in the hope that the bad-tempered sea god wouldn't hear.

King Cyzicus slapped Jason on the back, wished them all luck and set off back to the city. The Argonauts took their places on the damp rowing benches and Tiphys steered the *Argo* out of the harbour between the huge floating corpses, while the wedding party stood waving on the shore.

Once back out at sea, Nauplius, the navigator, set a course for the east. They sailed all afternoon without incident, but soon after sunset the wind veered, a storm started to blow up and the strong wind began to buffet the ship back to land.

"Poseidon must be angry," shouted Acastus above the noise of the gale. He was gripping the side of the ship and his face was deathly pale. "We'll just have to—"

He spun around, hung his head over the side of the ship and retched his portion of King Cyzicus's delicious wedding feast into the ocean with a loud "UUUUGH".

And Acastus was not the only one who was suffering. Most of the others were clinging to the benches with grim, green faces as the rain lashed down, the thunder roared and mountainous waves surged around them, wishing they hadn't indulged themselves quite so heavily at the wedding feast.

"I can't believe all this fuss," shouted Atalanta cheerfully to Heracles as she strode briskly up to the stern. A jagged fork of lightning slashed the sky and illuminated her healthy pink cheeks and glowing skin. "It's only a storm."

"Hmmm," was all that Heracles managed to say. Even he was clutching his stomach and his face was a delicate shade of green.

The *Argo* rolled wildly from side to side and finally was driven onto a beach in the pitch dark and pouring rain. Even Nauplius had no idea where they were. The storm-battered Argonauts grabbed their weapons and prepared to disembark.

For a few startling seconds the sound of the tempest was drowned out by a terrifying war cry which echoed around the beach. Then a hail of spears thudded into the deck.

"We're under attack!" called Atalanta for the second time that day.

Forgetting their seasickness, the Argonauts leaped down onto the beach to fend off their attackers. Spears and shields clashed together, a shower of arrows rained down and violent cries tore through the darkness.

Heracles rushed around in a blind frenzy, lashing out furiously at anyone who came near him. Body after body fell to the ground and soon the air was filled with the dying groans of the unknown warriors.

With a ferocious yell, Jason set upon the leader of the group, thrusting his spear straight through his enemy's heart. The man wailed, staggered back and plunged into a pool of seawater with a loud splash.

As soon as the remaining attackers realized their leader was dead, they dropped their weapons, turned tail and fled into the darkness.

The Argonauts spent a miserable night on the beach, sheltering as best they could from the storm, anticipating another attack at any minute, and wondering on whose godforsaken shores they had been washed up.

A piercing cry at first light gave them the answer. Jason awoke to see Castor running up the beach, weaving between piles of mangled bodies which were spread out on the sand like rotting seaweed. He was shouting and waving his arms around. His face was pale, his eyes wide with shock and clutched in his hand was what looked like a dripping wet animal skin.

"What is it, Castor?" asked Jason urgently.

"Cyzicus!" panted Castor. "King Cyzicus is dead!"

It took a few seconds for the truth to hit home – Castor was holding King Cyzicus's lion skin.

In the confusion of the storm, the *Argo* had been blown back to the land of the Dolionians and – Jason suddenly realized with a stab of desperate remorse – in the heat of the battle he had killed the king. The corpses which lay scattered all over the beach were just about all that was left of the group of Dolionians who had gathered on the shore to wave them off.

"No-ooo!" Jason screamed, sinking to his knees and beating the blood-soaked sand with his fists. Heracles ran over, placed his large hand on the younger man's shoulder and squeezed it gently.

"How were we to know?" was all he could think of to say.

Barricaded back inside their city, the few surviving Dolionian warriors were giving their account of the battle. As far as they knew, Cyzicus had met his death at the hands of marauding pirates on a night-time raid. It was only later, when the grief-stricken Argonauts arrived carrying the bodies of their comrades, that they realized what had really happened.

But it was too late to save Cleite, the king's new bride. As soon as she'd heard that her husband was dead, she had slipped secretly out to the forest, tied a rope around her neck and hanged herself from an oak tree.

Three days of mourning followed these events. The thunder and howling winds of the continuing storm were accompanied by the weeping of the Argonauts and Dolionians alike when

they buried Cyzicus and Cleite. Gods and goddesses came to grieve, and it is said that the wood sprites wept so despairingly for Cleite that their tears formed a spring which was named after her.

"Poseidon's mother, Rhea, sent a kingfisher with a message,"

And still the storm continued. For twelve more days and nights it raged while the Argonauts grew more and more frustrated. They had been there for weeks and still could not set sail. They said prayers to great Zeus, made offerings to Apollo and sacrifices to mighty Poseidon. But nothing worked. Who, or what could be causing the storm? Why did the winds never drop?

The explanation finally came in the dead of night when most of the Argonauts were asleep in the *Argo* and Acastus and Mopsus were keeping watch. All of a sudden a beautiful little bird appeared. It hovered momentarily above Jason's head before perching on the prow, where it sat twittering in a high, shrill voice. Mopsus stood listening, his head to one side, then darted over to Jason and shook him.

"I have a message for you," said Mopsus hurriedly, "a message from Rhea. She's very angry that you killed her brothers – that's why we're stuck here – she whipped up this storm to punish us."

"What are you talking about, Mopsus?" asked Jason irritably, rubbing his eyes.

said Mopsus, speaking as slowly and clearly as he could in his excitement. "It spoke to me just now – I can understand birds. You remember the six-armed giants?"

Jason nodded slowly.

"Well, they were her brothers, and when she found out we'd killed them, she conjured up this storm and drove us onto the beach."

"I see," said Jason.

"And she made sure Cyzicus was killed because *he* had killed her sacred lion when he was hunting on Mount Dindymum."

"So what can we do about it?" asked Jason, now fully awake and ready to try anything which might hasten their departure.

"Make a sacrifice to Rhea," was the reply.

By sunrise, a small procession of Argonauts was making its way up Mount Dindymum. Jason was leading an old goat behind him and Argus was carefully carving a piece of vine stump into the image of Rhea. This was placed on the altar that they built at the top of the mountain. As they poured wine on the altar, they called upon Rhea and implored her to calm the storm winds. Then they performed the sacrifice.

Hardly had the old goat drawn its last breath, when the gnarled mountain trees burst into blossom, a million flowers bloomed on the stony mountainside and a crystal clear stream gushed from the parched ground. And suddenly the wind dropped.

Rhea was satisfied.

As the sun rose, the Argonauts made their way back down the mountain. It was a fine spring morning. At last they could be on their way.

"I have an idea," said Heracles later when they were rowing through the calm waters of the Propontis.

"Well that must be an a lifetime first!" Orpheus said to Castor under his breath. Heracles was not famed for his intellect.

"And what might that be?" Jason asked.

"We could have a competition – see who can keep rowing the longest – it would be fun!" boomed Heracles.

"Well, all I can say is I hope no one expects *me* to join in," announced Orpheus.

Happily, the other Argonauts

were much more enthusiastic about Heracles's suggestion, and soon the *Argo* was flying through the water to the sound of Orpheus's lyre. Many strenuous hours later, only Jason and Heracles were left in the contest. The other defeated rowers lay slumped on their benches, exhausted.

Seated on opposite sides of the ship, Heracles and Jason continued to heave the *Argo* forward, though Jason was near to collapse. Finally, as they approached the mouth of the River Chius, he gave a groan of pain and frustration and fell back. Heracles had won! But just at that instant there was a loud *CRACK*. The huge man's oar snapped clean in two.

He lurched sideways, still pulling on the useless stump of his oar, while the blade was carried away by the current. Cursing loudly, he picked himself up, drew the stump through the oar hole and flung it down at his feet, while Jason lay sprawled on the deck, laughing and gasping for breath.

The others had now recovered enough to bring the boat onto a beach near the river. While they prepared their evening meal, Heracles, armed with an axe, went off into the forest to find some wood to make into a new oar and Hylas, his servant, set off with a pitcher to get water.

Two hours later Heracles was sitting on the beach holding his new oar, but Hylas had still not returned. A young rower called Polyphemus was sent to look for him. By now it was dark and Heracles was worried. Hylas was almost like a son to him and if anything had happened. . . He seized an oil lamp and plunged frantically back into the forest, bellowing "Hylas! Hylas!" at the top of his voice. His shouts were answered by Polyphemus who came running up to him.

"I found this," said the young man breathlessly, holding out Hylas's pitcher, "at the side of a pool."

Heracles groaned.

"There were no signs of a struggle or anything like that," reported Polyphemus. "If he'd been taken by an animal there would have been. . . "

"Blood," said Heracles, turning the pitcher over and over in his enormous calloused hands.

They found their way back to the pool and did their best by the dim light of the lamp to search the area. But there was no sign of Hylas. It was as if he'd vanished into thin air.

And indeed Hylas *was* far beyond their reach. When he had arrived at the pool it was just at the hour when all the nymphs gathered to sing songs to their goddess Artemis. Nymphs were beautiful young women with magical powers who lived in caves, woods and water. Many a mortal had succumbed to their charms.

Hylas knelt at the edge of the dappled water in the soft evening light just as the nymph of that pool was coming up to the surface. She looked up through the water at his handsome face and fell instantly in love. Hylas bent forward to fill his pitcher. The nymph's heart was pounding. His face was only inches away now. If she could just get him to come a little closer. . .

She stretched out her hands through the weeds, grabbed hold of his arms, and with one deft move tossed the pitcher onto the grass and drew him swiftly down to her, down through the slimy weeds, down through the swirling water, down to her watery domain in the depths of the pool. Hylas was never seen again.

Heracles and Polyphemus knew none of this as they ran back to the beach, shouting "Hylas! Hyyyy-las!" into the darkness. When they'd alerted the others, everyone spread out to look for the missing boy. All night long they searched, and most of the morning too. Heracles charged about like an angry bull, roaring in distress and calling his servant's name over and over again, but there was no response to his desperate cries.

"I'm not leaving without him," said Heracles stubbornly, when Jason gave orders to prepare to go.

"There's nothing more we can do," Jason replied gently. "We could search for days and still find no trace of him. I'm sorry Heracles, but I really have no choice."

Heracles's eyes filled with tears.

"I must at least find his body," he said despairingly. "I owe his mother that much."

When the *Argo* drew away from the beach, the famed demigod was still standing on the shore with his back to the sea, shouting "Hylas! Hylas!" into the unyielding air.

For the first time since they had left Iolcus, the Argonauts began to argue. Many of the younger ones started to accuse Jason, saying that he'd abandoned Heracles because he was jealous of him; that he wanted all the glory for himself; that Heracles should have been leader in the first place and that they should go back to the beach and persuade him to come back on board.

An angry young archer called Telamon rushed at Tiphys and tried to seize control of the helm, and he would have succeeded, had not Zetes and Calais darted down to restrain him.

The quarrel continued. Some of the Argonauts refused to row and picked up their weapons. Everybody started running around, shouting, and the *Argo* began drifting aimlessly, pitching from side to side.

Suddenly the waters at the stern parted. An enormous hand shot out of the sea and grabbed the back of the boat. It was followed by a huge, shaggy head and another hand holding a massive three-pronged spear. Then a gargantuan body emerged as far as the waist. A stunned silence gripped the crew. Everyone knew instantly who this was: the great god Poseidon himself.

"It is the will of Zeus," boomed the sea god. "And Zeus must be obeyed."

No one dared move a muscle nor say a word as his thunderous voice shook the ship.

"Jason is right. Heracles is destined for other tasks. Do not think *you* can decide his fate, foolish mortals."

The Argonauts cowered in the shadow of the god's colossal weapon which he was pointing straight at them.

"And as for Hylas," roared Poseidon. "He is the husband of a nymph now. He has been chosen. He will never return to you."

With these words, he let go of the stern and plunged head-first back into the sea. As his gigantic feet sank below the surface, an angry, swirling whirlpool appeared. The *Argo* was drawn towards it, slowly at first, moving round and round in wide circles, but then spinning faster and faster, out of control, into the seething vortex, plunging down, closer and closer to the whirling funnel that would consume the ship and splinter it into a million pieces.

Paralyzed by fear, the Argonauts could do nothing but watch helplessly as they were sucked in toward the merciless gaping mouth, sucked in to their doom in this yawning black hole. . .

All of a sudden, at the very brink of the abyss, the momentum was reversed and the *Argo* was spat out into the air. With a tumultuous splash, it landed back in the sea, stern-first, only to be caught by a mountainous wave which sent it shooting out over the ocean faster than an arrow in flight.

The Argonauts gripped their benches and clenched their teeth in terror. Someone started screaming. If they loosened their grip for even a second they would be catapulted into the air. Islands flashed past, barely visible through the wall of spray sent up on either side. Lynceus yelled. He had sighted land ahead of them.

Jason moaned in horror when he realized they were heading straight for it at breakneck speed. In a matter of seconds they would smash into the rocky beach and be pounded to smithereens by the surf. He shut his eyes and prayed.

At that same instant, the ship hit a breaking wave. The crew was hurled onto the deck in a chaotic, jumbled heap of bodies and weapons.

But the impact had slowed them down. The *Argo* drifted into the shore and creaked to a halt on the beach. The Argonauts began to disentangle their battered limbs and weapons. A relieved murmur swept through the crew, followed by hesitant, nervous laughter when they realized the nightmare was at last over and they had survived.

Poseidon had proved his point. They would never doubt Jason again.

. . . the great god Poseidon himself

Chapter five

THE CLASHING ROCKS

The *Argo* had been washed onto a windswept beach at the foot of a cliff, though the Argonauts scarcely had time to take this in because within seconds of their landing, a group of burly armed men were charging toward them over the sand, swearing and shouting and beating on their shields.

"Oh no!" said Jason to himself. His first reaction was to order the crew back on board and get away from the island as fast as he could, but the ship was in desperate need of repair, and within seconds the rowdy group was standing in a tight circle around them, looking, if it were at all possible, even more aggressive than Heracles in a bad mood.

Jason wished desperately that the great warrior was still with them when he turned to face the tall, thickset man who seemed to be the leader of the group.

"We are the Argona—"

"Fight, or I'll throw you over the cliff," barked the man. "I don't care who you are or where you've come from. This is *my* island. I am King Amycus and I WANT TO FIGHT!"

He was dangling a pair of leather boxing gloves from his outstretched hand and was clearly in no mood for a discussion.

Jason stared at him, too surprised to speak.

"I'll fight anyone you want," said the man gruffly, ramming the gloves into Jason's rib cage with such force that he was shunted back. "I've fought every man who has set foot on this island – and killed every one of them. No one beats me – ever."

Jason let out an involuntary sigh. He could hear Orpheus just behind him tutting disapprovingly and muttering "stupid oaf" under his breath.

"Not *afraid*, are you?" said the man in a mocking voice. "Not *afraid* of a little boxing match?"

His men all began to laugh contemptuously, throwing their heads back and guffawing loudly. Polydeuces made use of this distraction to ease his way through the crew to Jason's side.

"*I'll* do it," he whispered, below the noise of what was gradually turning into a chant of "Fight! Fight! Fight!"

Of course! thought Jason. Polydeuces had won the boxing contest at the Olympic Games.

Jason raised his hand for silence and addressed the man.

"I'm sure you'd prefer to fight a *good* boxer," he said.

"I've already told you – I'll fight anyone you want," said King Amycus, putting up his fists and stabbing the air with little punches. "I'm the boxing king and king of the boxers."

His men gave a cheer.

"Then you won't mind taking on my friend Polydeuces here," said Jason casually when the noise died down.

A few sharp intakes of breath could be heard at the mention of the champion's name.

"Er. . . no," said King Amycus, dropping his guard, suddenly not quite so confident.

"Usual rules?" asked Polydeuces.

"Rules!" snorted Amycus. "What are they?"

This facetious reply sent another wave of laughter surging through his men.

Polydeuces said nothing, but glared at his opponent and put on the gloves. From somewhere in the crowd the king's own gloves – twice the size and studded with bronze spikes – appeared. Polydeuces felt his knees weaken at the sight of them, but managed to keep his outward composure, even when Amycus stripped off his cloak to reveal his enormous, hairy torso.

The crowd shuffled back to make space for the two men, who began to pace around, eyeing each other savagely, like tigers in a cage. Amycus was by far the larger of the pair and it was he who tried to land the first blow – not a punch, but a bull-like charge in the direction of Polydeuces's stomach. The Argonaut saw it coming and dodged nimbly out of the way, sending the king hurtling head-first into the spectators with a furious, frustrated groan.

The big man quickly recovered his balance and spun around, teeth gritted and bared. His eyes shone wildly as he struck out again with a loud grunt, this time aiming directly for the Argonaut's face, but Polydeuces managed to duck just before the bronze spikes made contact with his nose, leaving the king's huge hand to smash into empty air.

Now it was the Olympic champion's turn to attack. Bobbing and weaving from side to side, he delivered a volley of punishing punches to the king's torso, followed by a sharp uppercut to the chin.

Amycus staggered back, reeling from the pain, but his opponent was upon him again with a stabbing right hook to the cheek and a swift left-handed punch to the stomach which knocked him off balance and sent him sprawling on the sand.

Amycus's men were horrified. They had never seen their leader losing. The Argonauts cheered ecstatically, and Castor, leaping and yelling in delight, rushed forward to congratulate his brother.

But Amycus wasn't ready to give in. Spurred on by the shouting, he hauled himself up off the ground, clenched his fists above his head like spiked horns, bent forward and, with a deafening bellow, charged at his opponent full tilt.

Polydeuces was thrown sideways by the impact, crying out in pain as the spikes pierced his flesh. The king's followers roared their approval and their leader, beaming from ear to ear, punched the air in an arrogant gesture of triumph.

Polydeuces caught his breath and with the Argonauts' shouts of encouragement ringing in his ears, launched himself at Amycus again with a series of accurate and perfectly timed

punches. He dodged and jabbed and ducked and hooked until the big man, too slow and lumbering to defend himself effectively, was spinning groggily.

Quick as a dragonfly and agile as a cat, Polydeuces darted dexterously around, delivering punch after punch to the king's head, which was rapidly turning into an unrecognizable mess of bruises, blood and broken teeth.

Mouths agape, the onlookers stood transfixed as though watching a fight between the gods themselves. Gasps of "OOH!" or "AAH!" could be heard each time one of the Argonaut's blows met its mark.

"Surrender!" Polydeuces shouted, but Amycus refused to give in. Blinded by the blood running down his face, he struck out aimlessly, arms flailing clumsily in the afternoon sunshine.

If Amycus had conceded at that point, he would have escaped with his life, but each time Polydeuces relaxed the onslaught and asked him if he'd had enough, some primitive, animal force took over and kept the big man on his feet, punching the air wildly. So Polydeuces had no choice but to continue, until one final pounding blow broke the king's skull.

Amycus sank to his knees. His great body swayed momentarily like a tree in the wind, then toppled forward, face-first, and hit the sand with a thud.

King Amycus was dead.

"Brilliant!" shouted Atalanta, helping to lift the champion onto his brother's shoulders. The Argonauts whooped with joy.

The king's followers just stared at their leader's body in stunned silence, then panic took over and they ran around in a frenzy, waving their spears and urging each other to attack the Argonauts. But Amycus's death had left no one in charge, and all it took was a thunderous victory cry from the Argonauts to send the whole disorderly rabble fleeing up the beach like startled rabbits.

The Argonauts congratulated Polydeuces and went off to find food and water and the materials they needed to repair the ship. While Castor carefully cleaned and dressed his brother's wounds, the others made a camp on the beach and it was there they spent a blissfully peaceful and undisturbed night.

When the *Argo* set sail early the next morning, King Amycus's body still lay slumped on the sand where he had fallen, like a beached whale. Jason surveyed it impassively from the stern as they drew away from the island.

Nauplius calculated that with a fair wind they should reach the eastern shore of the Propontis by nightfall. And he was right. The Argonauts made good speed to their next port of call, a city known as Salmydessus at the entrance to the Bosphorus, the narrow channel which connected the Propontis and the Black Sea.

Their hostile reception of the previous evening could not have contrasted more with the welcome awaiting them in Salmydessus. This city was ruled by King Phineus, a kind, skinny old man, who invited them all to his palace for a feast.

Phineus was blind. He told them he had chosen this affliction when the gods had given him the options of a short life or blindness as a punishment for foretelling the future too accurately. But his choice had enraged Helios, the sun god, who was offended that Phineus should have chosen a continual state of darkness over the sunlight he provided. And Helios had sent some terrible monsters called the Harpies to plague him.

As soon as Jason began to ask Phineus about the best way to get to Colchis, the old man said, "Rid me of the Harpies and then I'll tell you."

"What are the Harpies?" asked Jason.

"You'll soon see," was Phineus's reply.

They were sitting around an enormous table in the courtyard of the palace, and as they were talking, Phineus's servants began to bring in the meal. Plate after plate of luscious-looking food arrived on the table. The Argonauts eyed it hungrily.

"Outdoors or indoors – makes no difference," said Phineus mysteriously. "They always arrive."

All of a sudden a horrible screeching filled the air, and out of the sky dropped two winged shapes. At first Jason thought they were birds, but Mopsus knew better – they spoke no language he could understand and were clearly like nothing he had seen before, with their hideous female faces and long, sharp claws.

They descended on the table in a flurry of feathers and squawking, devouring anything they could lay their hands on and – much worse – covering everything they didn't eat in foul, stinking droppings, so that it was instantly inedible.

"Filthy scavengers!" shouted Phineus. He grabbed his staff and swept it across the table, but the Harpies had already taken flight, disappearing into the evening air with screaming cries, as swiftly as they'd arrived.

"Those are the Harpies," said Phineus sadly. "Now you see my problem."

While an army of servants filed in to clear up the mess, King Phineus described his daily ordeal: "Every

"Filthy scavengers!" shouted Phineus

single meal, it's always the same. The Harpies arrive from nowhere and snatch the food from under my very nose. For years and years, I've had to fight for every morsel. You wouldn't believe how much food they've ruined, and how little I've managed to eat! I've prayed to the gods and made all sorts of offerings to Helios, but they show no mercy, even to an old blind man. My one wish is to be able sit down and eat a meal in peace, without constant interruptions from those verminous creatures."

As he was speaking, the servants were disposing of the sullied remains of the meal, scraping droppings and spoiled food into pails and vigorously scrubbing down the long table.

"We've tried catapults. . . bows and arrows. . . cats and traps. . . poisoned bait, but nothing deters them – nothing – they're just too fast, and immune to poison!"

The old man's unseeing eyes filled with tears of frustration. Jason laid a comforting hand on his shoulder and motioned to Zetes and Calais, the winged sons of the North Wind.

"Ask your servants to bring in some more food," he said to Phineus. We'll see what we can do."

The table was now clear again, and Phineus ordered another meal. While it was being prepared, Zetes and Calais exercised their wings and sharpened their swords.

The Clashing Rocks

When the Harpies appeared this time, the twins were ready, flying up to meet them, swords in hand, before the monsters could get anywhere near the table. The Harpies' screeching was deafening and they lashed out savagely with their claws, but the twins were expert swordsmen, and within seconds the monsters had taken flight, screeching loudly. Zetes and Calais chased them high into the air and drove them far from the palace and out across the sea.

Much later, the Argonauts learned that Phineus was never troubled by the Harpies again. Now, for the first time in years, he sat down to an undisturbed meal and between great mouthfuls of food, gratefully explained to the Argonauts all the things they needed to know: how to navigate the Bosphorus and pass safely through the Clashing Rocks; what they might encounter on the Island of Ares; how to avoid the treacherous reefs and sandbanks of the Black Sea, and the best route to Colchis.

When he'd eaten his fill, Phineus left the courtyard and returned a few minutes later clutching a small basket.
"Remember," he said, handing it to Jason, "get as close as you can to the rocks before you open it, then follow through on the rebound."
Jason nodded.

"Trust in Athene!" were Phineus's parting words. Then he wished them luck, said goodbye and went off to bed, patting his full stomach contentedly.

Even today the Bosphorus is known for its fierce, erratic currents, which can catch ships in eddies, whirl them around like toys and smash them into the banks. But having survived this ordeal, modern sailors do not then have to face the Symplegades, or Clashing Rocks, as the Argonauts did the following afternoon.

The Symplegades guarded the entrance to the Black Sea, and no one before had ever succeeded in passing through them. They were two enormous boulders which were not attached to the seabed, but crashed together unpredictably, crushing ships as they collided and flinging up a seething, roaring mass of sea water.

Already tired after rowing through the Bosphorus, the Argonauts did not immediately identify the ominous booming sounds which greeted them when they approached the Black Sea. Then two huge, dark shapes loomed into view through the mist, and the rowers watched in awe as the dreaded rocks clashed together with a thunderous roar.

Atalanta quickly ran to the stern and found the basket that Phineus had given them. Inside it was a white dove. Remembering the blind king's words,

Tiphys steered the *Argo* in as close to the Clashing Rocks as possible, then Atalanta opened the basket and released the dove into the air. It flew between the boulders which came hurtling together with an ear-splitting *CRASH*, but the dove was already through, sacrificing only a couple of tail feathers on the way.

Now, while the boulders were on the rebound, it was the *Argo's* turn. The current was so strong and the swell so great, the rowers could scarcely control the ship as they heaved it into the rocks' gaping jaws. The water surged around them. Foam from mountainous waves was hurled high above their heads. Timbers creaked. The rowers strained and Jason yelled. The rocks were moving in again, coming closer and closer. The gap was narrowing rapidly.

"Faster!" shouted Tiphys, but his voice was drowned out by the waves crashing over them. The rowers groaned, tearing muscles and grinding bones to drag the oars through the foaming water. The boulders were just inches away now. Any second the ship would be smashed to pieces. Orpheus screamed.

Louder than a thunderclap, the colossal rocks clashed violently together. The earth shook, the sea boiled and enormous lumps of rock rained down into the water.

But somehow the *Argo* was safely through, although a shattered carving on her stern showed how close they had come to calamity.

The rowers sat back and recovered their breath as the ship drifted gently out into the Black Sea. The Argonauts were the very first sailors ever to pass through the Clashing Rocks and live to tell the tale.

Jason said a prayer of thanks to Athene.

Up on Mount Olympus, the goddess awoke with a start. Someone was calling her name. She looked down and saw Jason standing at the prow of his battered ship.

"I'm so sorry young man," she said out loud, "but you caught me napping." She yawned noisily and stretched her arms. "You got through that one all by yourself – nothing to do with me. It's just I've been so busy lately and. . . well, I must take better care of you in the future. Now let me see if I can fix that irritating little noise."

Down on the *Argo*, Jason suddenly realized that the booming sound had ceased. Looking back, he saw that the Clashing Rocks were standing still, rooted firmly in the positions where Athene had now planted them, never to move again.

Chapter six

ARRIVAL AT COLCHIS

I f Athene hadn't fallen asleep again, perhaps disaster wouldn't have struck that evening on a quiet riverbank near the Black Sea coast. But the goddess's usually watchful eyes were shut tight when the Argonauts came to shore and found what looked like a peaceful spot to recover their strength.

Idmon and Idas, two of the younger Argonauts, volunteered to get water, so they grabbed a pitcher and set off for the river. They were tramping through a reed bed, when Idmon heard a rustling noise. Before he knew what was happening, an enormous wild boar was charging straight at him.

Idas watched in horror as the ferocious creature drove its tusks into Idmon's legs, then turned around and trotted off nonchalantly into the reeds. Idmon was screaming with pain. Idas started yelling for help, but the beast was undeterred. Within seconds it was rushing at the wounded man again.

This time Idas was ready. He met the boar head on and thrust his spear deep into its heart. The giant creature squealed and toppled to the ground where it took its last breath.

But it was too late for Idmon. By the time the other Argonauts arrived, he had already lost so much blood, there was nothing they could do to save him. Jason silently cursed whichever god or goddess had let this happen. But no one on Mount Olympus took heed, and Athene must still have been sleeping, for later that day tragedy struck again.

In the early afternoon, Tiphys, the pilot, had begun to feel ill, and by nightfall he had a fever. If they'd been back among the familiar fields and mountains of Greece, Jason would have known which herbs to gather to treat him, but here on a remote beach, he could only watch powerlessly as Tiphys writhed and moaned in pain and then sank into unconsciousness.

Just before dawn, the pilot died.

It was a sorrowful band of Argonauts that rowed back out to sea. They had performed the funeral rites as best they could and Orpheus had played a lament while they wept around the makeshift graves of their comrades. Now no one could think of anything to say to relieve the misery, so they just concentrated on rowing and then continued east under sail.

They sailed past the land of the Amazons, a race of fierce female warriors, and close to the coast of a country where people lived in small wooden castles. Near sunset, Lynceus spotted a small rocky island, and Ancaeus, who had been chosen to replace Tiphys as pilot, brought them safely in to the shore.

That night there was a terrible storm. The wind raged and howled and a drenching rain lashed down. In the middle of the night, the few Argonauts who had managed to get to sleep were woken by shouts from the beach. They all rushed down to see four bedraggled men scrambling out of the waves.

When they had recovered enough to speak, the men explained that they were the survivors of a shipwreck, who had managed to save themselves from drowning by clinging to pieces of the wreckage. By a strange coincidence, it turned out that they were the sons of Chalciope and Phrixus – who, when he was a boy, had ridden to Colchis on the back of the golden ram. Their father was now dead and they had been on their way from Colchis to Greece to claim their grandfather's

kingdom, when their ship had been hit by the storm.

Four new crew members who knew their way to Colchis seemed like a gift from the gods to Jason – perhaps they were – and the men needed little encouragement to join the crew. In fact they had no choice, other than being stranded on a rocky island without a ship, food or weapons.

The storm soon passed and the Argonauts were greeted by a cloudless sky when they prepared to set sail the next morning. But they were only a few yards from shore when the sky suddenly darkened again. This time it was not storm clouds almost blotting out the sun, but some large, dark ragged shapes. The Argonauts had been through so much since they left King Phineus's palace, it took a while for them to realize what the shapes were. Atalanta remembered first.

"The Stymphalian birds!" she cried, looking up at the flock of massive winged creatures. Phineus had warned them that these man-eating monsters with their sharp bronze beaks and feathers were roosting on the Island of Ares and were likely to attack.

"Helmets and shields!" called Jason, suddenly recalling Phineus's advice, just as the first metal feather dropped from the sky and slashed through the sail.

"OW!" yelled a rower called Oileus as the tip of another stabbed his shoulder.

The Argonauts grabbed their helmets and weapons, and while some rowed, others shouted and banged their shields together above their heads. Atalanta shot volley after volley of arrows at the birds. Each time she as quickly as they had arrived, Atalanta had deprived the flock of fourteen members.

The female archer was congratulated. Apart from the wound to Oileus's shoulder and the damaged sail, they had survived the attack remarkably unscathed. Now, as far as they knew,

scored a hit, a gleaming body plunged into the sea with a loud SPLASH! and the Argonauts cheered.

When the birds finally took flight, disappearing off into the clear blue sky no more dangers lay between them and Colchis. The object of their quest was as good as in sight.

On Mount Olympus, Hera and Athene were having a meeting.

"They'll need some help, poor things," said Hera sadly, looking down at the *Argo* with its tattered sail and weary crew.

"Yes," agreed Athene, "that awful King Aites won't just hand over the Golden Fleece and let them sail off with it."

"We need a plan," said Hera decisively, but then fell silent and stared at the floor, because she couldn't think of one.

Both goddesses were feeling rather guilty. They had vowed to help and protect Jason, but lately they'd been so busy or tired, they just hadn't had time to watch over him. He'd nearly been crushed by the Clashing Rocks, and the moment they had turned their backs it seemed that the crew had started dropping like flies – that business with the wild boar had been dreadful. There must be no more mistakes.

"Eros!" said Hera, suddenly inspired.

"Who?" replied Athene.

"You know – that naughty little son of Aphrodite's – the one who causes all the trouble with his love arrows."

"But how can he help?" asked Athene.

"For a goddess of wisdom, you can be remarkably slow sometimes," said Hera rudely.

"And for queen of the gods, you are a very poor communicator," Athene snapped back, adding, "I'm sorry, but it just seems to me that love is the very last thing Jason needs right now."

"Yes, but he does need an ally," explained Hera, as patiently as she could. "Someone with inside knowledge at the palace, and I think I know just the woman for the job."

"You don't mean – what's her name? Aites's daughter – that witch with all the potions and lotions – you know – MEDEA!" said Athene.

"Why not?" said Hera, enjoying watching Athene's surprised reactions as her plan unfolded. "If anyone knows Colchis, then she does, and what better way to help Jason than to make her fall so head-over-heels in love with him that she'll do anything he asks?"

"Brilliant!" gasped Athene.

They went straight to Aphrodite who said she would do her best to persuade Eros to perform the task.

When she found her son, he was playing dice with his friend Ganymede. Eros was winning, but only, as usual, by cheating.

"Why should I?" said the spoiled boy, when his mother had explained that she wanted him to shoot an arrow at Medea so she would fall in love with Jason.

"Because, my darling, if you do, I'll give you this," said Aphrodite, proffering a golden ball striped with blue enamel. "It belonged to Zeus when he was a little boy. Look what it can do."

She threw the ball to Ganymede. It streaked through the air, leaving a sparkling trail, like a shooting star. Eros clapped his hands in delight.

"I'll do it," he said.

"Right in the heart, mind you," said Aphrodite. "There'll be no reward for a botched job."

Meanwhile, the Argonauts were rowing up the River Phasis on their way to Colchis. Before they came within sight of the city, Jason ordered the *Argo* to be moored in a calm backwater where it was almost hidden by reeds. It was time to come up with a plan.

Jason suggested that he should go to King Aites' palace with Phrixus's sons, who were the king's grandsons, and simply ask the king if he could have the Golden Fleece. Only if Aites refused, would he resort to "more direct methods". Everyone thought this was a good idea, so Jason and his four companions set off.

When they approached the palace, the first person they met was Chalciope, who was very surprised to see her four sons back so soon. When she had heard their story, she thanked Jason profusely for having rescued them, and said she would do her best to help persuade her father to hand over the fleece.

As soon as King Aites saw Jason, he scowled angrily. This was one thing he had not expected – a strange young Greek in his palace – surely King Laomedon of Troy had vowed to prevent all Greeks from entering the Black sea? How on earth had this one slipped through the Hellespont?

"What are you doing back here so soon?" he asked his grandsons. Aegeus – the youngest and the one Aites liked best – began to explain. He said that they owed their lives to Jason who had come all the way from Greece to get the Golden Fleece and please could Aites hand it over?

Aites looked furious. He stepped down from his chair, circled Jason like a prowling wolf, and then he gave a loud, contemptuous laugh.

"GIVE you the fleece?" he roared. "GIVE you the fleece? You must be joking!"

He thrust his face close to Jason's own and poked his finger into his ribs.

"GET – OUT – OF – MY – *SIGHT!*" he bellowed, stressing each word with a sharp prod.

"Go back to where you came from before I cut out your tongue and slice off your hands!"

"But sir—"

Just at that moment Medea walked in. The very instant she caught sight of Jason, she felt a sharp little stab in her heart and gasped. This was the most handsome and wonderful man she had ever seen in her life! A god among men!

It was love at first sight. She was totally stricken, completely and utterly besotted and head-over-heels in love. She would do anything to be with this man. Absolutely anything.

Eros's aim had been perfect.

Then Medea saw her father's scowling face and heard the desperate pleas of the gorgeous young man – he had come hundreds of miles; survived whirlpools, monsters, battles, storms. He would do anything to get the fleece. Anything.

That was when Medea intervened. She begged her father to help the young man. Then her sister, Chalciope, joined in too, along with the four grandsons, who reminded the king that they might not be alive that day if it weren't for Jason and his crew.

Wondering what all the noise was about, Medea's younger brother, Apsyrtus, also appeared on the scene and stood behind a column, watching quietly.

At first Aites looked as if he would not be swayed. Then a broad smile spread across his face. He walked back over to his chair and sat down, scratching his chin thoughtfully. The room fell silent.

Aites rubbed his hands together as he spoke.

"You can have the fleece," he said calmly, "if you complete a task."

Jason opened his mouth to respond, but Aites raised his hand to silence him.

"In the Field of Ares," he continued, "not far from this palace, two bulls run free. Anyone who has seen them will tell you they are unlike any other bulls in the world, for they were made by Hephaestus, the blacksmith of the gods. Their hooves are made of bronze and they breathe fire. Nobody has ever managed to harness them, but that is what you must do – yoke them together, then till the Field of Ares and sow it with dragons' teeth. Then, and only then, can you have the fleece."

Jason looked around the room. Every face seemed to be urging him to accept. Yet it was an impossible task for a mortal to perform. . . Then his eyes met Medea's. Something in her imploring gaze made him powerless to refuse. Reluctantly, he turned back to face Aites.

"I'll complete your task," he said confidently, "if it means you will let me have the fleece."

"Of course I will," Aites said, certain that Jason would fail.

Later that evening, Chalciope came to summon Jason to Medea's room. She had agreed to introduce her sister to the handsome young prince. Jason eagerly complied.

"My sister has. . . How can I put this? Let's just say, she has 'special powers.'" said Chalciope as they were crossing the courtyard. "She thinks she can help you."

"'Special powers' – what do you mean?" asked Jason.

"You'll soon find out," was all she would say.

In Medea's room, Jason was met by a warm smile and an almost overpowering herbal fragrance. He caught a sudden whiff of something sweet and woody that reminded him of Chiron's cave, but the other smells were unfamiliar. The room was crammed with bottles and jars, branches, twigs and bunches of dried flowers and leaves. In the corner stood a big bronze cauldron full of bubbling black liquid.

"You're a. . . a witch!" said Jason, suddenly realizing what Chalciope had meant by 'special powers'.

"You *could* call me that," said Medea, fluttering her eyelashes, "though I prefer 'sorceress' myself – it sounds a little more glamorous, somehow."

Jason went over to the cauldron and peered at its contents. He bent down to sniff it, then jumped back, gagging from the stink.

"Dragon's blood," said Medea. "They told me it was fresh, but I'm not so sure – smells a little off to me."

"Tell Jason why you've summoned him," said Chalciope rather brusquely. She knew her sister would spend all evening flirting if she had the chance and would never get to the point.

"I can help you," said Medea in a businesslike manner, "but you have to agree to my conditions."

"And what might they be?" said Jason distractedly. He was reading the labels on a row of jars:

TOADS' EYES
MEDIUM STRENGTH

POWDERED UNICORN HORN
APPLY SPARINGLY

HARPIES' TONGUES
KEEP OUT OF THE REACH
OF CHILDREN

"Take me back to Greece and marry me," said Medea.

"Excuse me?" said Jason, thinking he must have misheard.

"I can help you harness the bulls and get the fleece, but if I do, I want you to take me back to Greece in your ship and marry me."

Jason stood rooted to the spot, too surprised to speak.

"A fine, handsome young man like you must be in need of a wife," Medea purred, sidling up to him and running her hands over his leopard skin cloak. "And when you get home, and your uncle makes you king, you'll need a queen – a beautiful queen – a *powerful* queen."

The scents in the room seemed to be getting stronger. Jason was starting to feel lightheaded and almost overwhelmed by the perfume. All he could hear was Medea's entrancing voice. All he could see were her alluring green eyes, appealing lips and lustrous, long hair. Once again he was powerless to refuse.

"Yes," he said softly. "I'll marry you."

"Good," said Medea, smiling. "Then let's get to work."

She walked over to a shelf of bottles and ran the long, painted nail of her index finger slowly along them, checking the labels, one by one.

"Here it is," she said briskly, removing a bottle of blood-red liquid. "It's meant for fire-breathing dragons, but I'm fairly sure it will work against bulls too."

She pulled out the stopper and sniffed the contents. A new, even stronger smell pervaded the room.

A new, even stronger smell pervaded the room

"We have that poor man Prometheus to thank for this," she explained. "Have you heard of him?"

"Well, er. . . yes. . . some time ago," spluttered Jason, still too stunned to talk properly.

"When he stole fire from the gods," she continued authoritatively, as she measured out the potion, drop by careful drop, into a smaller bottle, "he was chained to a mountain as a punishment. And all day and every day he had his liver torn out by an eagle – it kept regrowing you see."

She stoppered the bottle and shook it vigorously, then held it up to the light.

"That should do it," she said assuredly. "Where was I? Oh yes – where the poor tortured man's blood spilled onto the ground, some yellow crocuses sprouted, and from the red stamens of those flowers, I made this potion – the only known protection from dragon's breath," she added proudly, handing the bottle to Jason.

"Rub it on your clothes, your weapons and every inch of exposed skin. Then you can tackle those bulls."

"Thank you," said Jason feebly, cradling the bottle in his palm.

Chalciope was now at his elbow, guiding him gently to the door.

"Oh, I almost forgot," called Medea. Jason turned around.

"You'll need these."

She stretched up and pulled down a large, dusty leather bag from a top shelf. Its contents rattled as she threw it to Jason.

"Dragons' teeth," she said. "Some of Cadmus's leftovers when he had—"

"Medea!" said Chalciope in exasperation. "We do *not* have all night."

"Never mind – I'll tell you that story another time. Just remember to throw the bag at the men."

"Er. . . yes," said Jason. He had no idea what she was talking about.

"Good luck, my darling," said Medea, blowing him a kiss before she closed the door.

Chapter seven

THE GOLDEN FLEECE

Medea's magic potion smelled disgusting and stung his eyes, but Jason tried not to let this distract him as he smeared it all over his body, clothes and weapons early the next morning. He had to concentrate on the task in hand.

The Field of Ares was on the side of a steep, grassy hill, only a short walk from the palace. When he reached it, there was no sign of the fire-breathing bulls, just a group of spectators who had gathered near the gate and were chattering excitedly. Jason strode confidently past them into the field, dragging the tilling blades behind him and carrying a spear, an enormous shield, the bag of dragon's teeth and a heavy bronze yoke from which trailed a wooden pole.

"Good luck!" called one of the onlookers, knowing full well that all the others who had stepped through that gate had been swiftly reduced to a heap of charred bones.

A little way into the field, Jason stuck the spear into the ground and left everything but the shield on the grass beside it. Then he began to climb the hill.

The air was already warm, and he soon worked up a sweat. Raising his hand to wipe his brow, he remembered, just in time, not to rub off the potion. If the magic didn't work, he would be. . . but there was no time to think about that now, because the noise started.

At first it was just a low rumbling coming from the other side of the hill, like waves breaking on a distant shore, but it soon turned into a heavy rhythmic pounding that shook the ground. Jason scanned the horizon. There was nothing to see, but the noise was getting louder.

He planted his feet firmly apart, held his shield out in front of his body and fixed his eyes on the top of the hill. His heart was thumping. His mouth had gone dry.

A terrifying bellowing filled the air and a fiery cloud of dust appeared. Jason gulped. Moments later two massive bulls stormed over the hill in a thunderous tumult of flames, fury and flying bronze hooves.

Jason clenched his teeth and locked his knees and elbows. The savage beasts were charging straight at him, snorting out great tongues of flame. He screwed up his eyes as the heat blasted his skin. There was a strange prickling – but no pain. The potion was working!

The grass at his feet burst into flames with an angry hiss. Someone in the crowd shrieked to warn him – the fire was licking his legs and creeping up to his tunic. But Jason did not move, even as a smell of burning filled his nostrils. He was mesmerized by the creatures' malevolent blood-red eyes, and the huge horns hurtling toward him.

He took a deep breath and braced himself. The fire engulfed him and at the same instant, with an ear-splitting crash that jolted every bone in his body, the two massive pairs of horns smashed into his shield.

The sound of the impact rang around the field. The crowd groaned, certain that the collision and the inferno had finished him off and that soon he'd be burned to a cinder – a great plume of black smoke rose high into the sky as if to confirm it. Convinced they'd seen the last of him, some turned to leave.

An amazed cry of "Look!" brought them running back. The enormous fireball that enveloped Jason

and the bulls had begun to move! Peering through the thick smoke and roaring flames, they could just about make out a shadowy figure holding the bulls by the horns and dragging them down the hill. Jason was alive!

Grunting with the super-human effort needed to control the raging beasts, he was forcing them slowly down to where he had left the yoke. They were bellowing furiously, digging their hooves into the scorched earth and lashing out at him viciously with their flaming breath, but he did not let go until the very moment when he was close enough to the yoke to grab it. Then with one deft move, he released the bulls, snatched up the yoke and threw it over the top of their horns and onto their necks. The stunned creatures stood rooted to the spot, rolling their eyes and shooting fire in frenzied snorts.

Jason worked quickly. He bound the yoke securely to their necks and hooked the yoke pole onto the metal tilling blades. Racing around to the back, he seized his spear, and with a quick prod, set the bulls in motion. The group at the gate could hardly believe their eyes. Jason had yoked the fire-breathing bulls and was tilling the Field of Ares! Someone ran off to alert the king.

It took Jason most of the rest of the day, toiling in the blazing sun, to finish the work. If he relaxed for even a second, the bulls might bolt. If he left even a tiny fragment of the vast field untouched, Aites would accuse him of not completing the task. The crowd grew bored of watching and drifted away.

When Aites was told about what had happened, he immediately went to the field to see if it were true. For a while he watched Jason doggedly toiling in the midday sun, and smiled to himself. This brave young Greek might have survived the fury of the bulls, but he had no idea what lay in store for him when he sowed the dragons' teeth. Nobody could survive that.

Near sunset Jason turned his last furrow, released the weary bulls, which stomped off over the brow of the hill, and then, close to exhaustion himself, began to scatter the contents of the leather bag which Medea had given him over the freshly dug soil.

He had sown about two-thirds of the field when he realized that the "seeds" were beginning to sprout. All he could see at first were sharp triangular-shaped shoots shining in the sun's setting rays. *What extraordinary plants!* he thought and continued sowing. When he turned around again the shoots were above the ground on the end of long straight stalks.

With an astonished gasp Jason realized they were the tops of spears! Spears were sprouting from the earth!

He hurriedly finished the sowing, threw the empty bag to the ground and sat down by the gate to watch. The sprouting spears were soon followed by the gleaming tops of helmets. Jason's astonishment was replaced by fear the instant the first head appeared. It was followed by another, and another and another.

Every face turned slowly to glare at him. Every mouth was set in a savage snarl, and when the hands appeared they waved the spears at him menacingly. Angry armed men were growing from the ground and every single one of them seemed intent on slaughtering him!

He had to think quickly. The men were now yelling and shouting and beating on their shields. Any minute their legs and feet would emerge and then they'd be free to come after him. He thought about making a run for it, but where could he hide from hundreds of men? He thought about trying to cut them down before they had fully emerged, but there were so many he would never succeed.

By the time the first pair of knees appeared, the noise was deafening. Jason tried to concentrate, but his tired brain was filled with the insistent beating of spears on shields and blood-curdling war cries. He stood at the gate, watching helplessly as feet began to form. Still no plan came to mind. Now they were taking their first steps,

The savage beasts were charging straight at him. . .

. . . snorting out great tongues of flame

Now the whole army was marching down the field, shouting at the top of their lungs and brandishing their spears. Powerless to defend himself, Jason closed his eyes and prayed for a swift end. . .

"Use the bag!" said a voice in his ear. Jason opened his eyes and looked around. There was no one there, but he recognized Medea's voice. Almost too late he realized what she meant. Darting over to where the bag lay, he snatched it up and flung it as hard as he could into the middle of the advancing soldiers. In an instant they stopped in their tracks, then in a demonic frenzy of clashing shields and spears, turned to attack one another.

Overwhelmed by exhaustion and relief, Jason sank to the ground and watched the army destroy itself. When he finally left the field in the deepening twilight, hundreds of lifeless bodies lay silhouetted against the blood-red sky at the top of the ridge and scattered like confetti over the freshly dug earth.

As he dragged himself back to the *Argo* through the thickening gloom, he frightened a man on the riverbank with his filthy, bedraggled appearance and maniacal grin. He was footsore, aching in every limb and totally drained of energy, but he felt more elated than ever before in his life. He had completed the task. The Golden Fleece would soon be his.

"Alive!" screamed Aites the next morning. "Alive! What do you mean he's alive?"

"Well, I saw him last night, sir, heading out along the riverbank," said the messenger. "Gave me a fright, sir, I can tell you, looming out of the darkness, all covered in soot and grinning from ear to—"

"That'll be enough, man," snapped the king, dismissing him with a peremptory wave of his hand. "Tell Medea I want to speak to her," he said to one of the maids. "Tell her I have a plan."

When Jason, Orpheus and Atalanta approached the palace later that morning, Medea was waiting outside the gates, clutching a branch in her hand. As soon as she saw Jason, she rushed up to him.

"My darling, listen," she said. "There's not a second to lose. We must go straight to the Grove of Ares and get the fleece and—"

"Hold on," said Jason, "I'm on my way to see your father. I completed the task – he's going to *give* me the fleece."

"NO!" said Medea firmly. "He's going to *kill* you – *and* all the Argonauts. And he's going to burn the *Argo*, he told me himself, not five minutes ago."

As she spoke, Medea was pulling Jason away from the palace. Atalanta

and Orpheus followed. Soon they were all walking at a brisk pace into the forest. No one had noticed a small figure slip out of the gates behind them.

"He lied to you about the fleece, don't you see?" continued Medea in an anguished voice. "He thought the bulls or the soldiers would finish you off. He was *furious* when he found out you were alive."

"Run back to the *Argo* as fast as you can," said Jason to Atalanta. "Tell them to row along the river and moor as close as possible to the Grove of Ares."

"Consider it done," said Atalanta, delighted that there was some action at last. She raced off, leaving a cloud of dust in her wake.

The others kept walking at the same brisk pace while Medea told them more about Aites's plan. All of a sudden Jason came to an abrupt halt.

"Wait a minute," he said, seizing hold of Orpheus's arm. "How do we know if we can trust her? This could be a trap."

Medea stopped and looked back at him, stunned by his words.

"If I wished you harm," she said quietly, "I could easily have made sure you were savaged by the bulls – or slaughtered by the soldiers in the Field of Ares." She moved closer to Jason and looked him in the eye.

"I swear," she said imploringly, "that I am trying to save your life. If you choose to ignore my help, then I don't give much for your chances."

She sounded so hurt that Jason felt ashamed he'd doubted her. He opened his mouth to apologize, but just at that moment Medea shrieked over his shoulder: "What, in the name of Zeus, are *you* doing here?"

Jason spun around. A small figure was trying to hide in a bush by the side of the track.

"Who is he?" asked Jason.

"My vile little brother," said Medea, hauling Apsyrtus out of the bush by his arm. The boy was squealing with laughter.

"I followed you from the palace!" he declared. "And nobody noticed."

"Well I've noticed now," said Medea crossly, "and you're to go home immediately."

"I don't want to," he said stubbornly, "and if you make me, I'll tell Dad where you are."

"Little brat!" said Medea.

"Old witch!" said her brother.

They had no choice but to let Apsyrtus come with them. He trotted along behind them as, hurrying through the forest to the Grove of Ares, Medea explained her plan.

A horrible loud hissing told them they had reached their destination. Crouching behind a bush at the edge of a clearing, they peered through the leaves at a vast oak tree

which stood in the middle, surrounded by skulls and bones.

"Wow!" whispered Apsyrtus when an enormous scaly dragon slithered down the tree. It was longer than the *Argo*, with huge snake-like jaws that gaped open to reveal rows of needle-sharp fangs. A forked red tongue flicked in and out menacingly. Jason stared hypnotically at the unblinking yellow eyes, until something glinting high in the tree, caught his eye. The Golden Fleece! He gazed in silent wonder at the long-sought object of his quest, shining like a beautiful golden cloud among the branches. All he had to do now was to get it down. Only a dragon stood in his way. . . an enormous deadly poisonous dragon.

The sound of music broke his trance. Above the noise of the hissing, he could hear Orpheus playing his lyre. Soon Medea joined in, singing a melodious song to charm the dragon to sleep. Jason found himself being lulled into a drowsy state by the music, but just in time shook himself awake. It was time to face the dragon.

The hissing had begun to subside when Medea and Jason moved slowly out into the clearing. Jason was armed with a shield and a sword. Medea carried just a juniper branch, but she kept singing her bewitching song.

As they approached the dragon, it lunged forward, but then reeled and swayed, as if fighting sleep. Still singing, Medea darted in front of Jason and flicked the branch at its lidless eyes. Sparkling drops of liquid flew through the air. The dragon drew back its head. Medea flicked again.

The enormous head began to weave from side to side, powerless to resist the potion with which she had drenched the branch. Orpheus strummed, Medea sang and flicked a third time. The dragon opened its jaws even wider in a gaping yawn, then its huge head slumped to the ground with a thud.

"Quick!" whispered Medea. "The magic won't last long and I've no more potion."

As fast as he could, Jason climbed up the dragon's nose, over its head, along its back and up into the tree. Balancing precariously on a mossy branch, he made his way, step by careful step, up to the Golden Fleece, shielding his eyes from its dazzling brilliance.

"Hurry!" called Medea from below in a low whisper. Jason stretched out his arm and touched the thick golden wool. It was soft and warm. A tingle of excitement ran down his spine. At last he had his hands on the Golden Fleece! Suddenly he heard the dragon hissing softly below him.

"Come *on!*" said Medea frantically. "It's waking up!"

Jason grabbed the edge of the fleece and dragged it to him. It was heavier than he expected. He bundled it up in his arms, turned around, and worked his way back along the branch as quickly as he could. The dragon was hissing groggily. Jason bounded down its back, onto its head and jumped to the ground just before it reared its sleepy head.

mouth gaping. Apsyrtus squealed in terror. They launched themselves over the bush, just as the jaws snapped shut. The dragon recoiled in disgust, spitting out a mouthful of leaves and twigs, along with a piece of Medea's skirt.

"Run!" screamed Medea. The huge jaws were opening, ready to swoop down and swallow them whole. Jason and Medea raced across the clearing in the direction of their companions, treading bones and skulls underfoot. The dragon lunged at them,

Medea had landed just inches from her brother. She grabbed him by the arm and with a shout of "MOVE!" hauled him through the trees in the direction of the river. Apsyrtus was shaking with fear. The others sprinted along behind. They could all hear a noise more frightening than the hissing of the dragon – galloping hooves and clanking weapons. Soldiers on horseback were on their trail.

As he ran, Jason prayed that Atalanta had reached the *Argo* safely. Otherwise they stood no chance. The sound of the soldiers was getting closer. He didn't dare look behind, but he could hear the horses' hooves crunching through the clearing. A terrified, muffled scream told him that one of the men had become the dragon's next meal, but the rest were still hard on his heels.

Medea was charging along in front of him, half carrying and half dragging her terrified brother.

"Faster!" she panted above the pounding hoofbeats. She raced out of the forest into bright sunshine. An expanse of water stretched before her – only a stone's throw away. And there at the riverbank was the *Argo*, sail raised, rowers at the ready.

When, seconds later, Jason appeared, the Argonauts cheered. Then they saw the sweat pouring down his face and the fear in his eyes, and realized he was running for his life. A moment later the source of his terror came galloping into view – a dozen armed men, spears held high, above their heads, ready to attack.

Suddenly Jason tripped. The fleece went flying through the air. He crashed to the ground and rolled over to see a horseman towering over him, spear in hand, face set in a furious, blood-thirsty scowl. Now the man was drawing back his arm, taking aim and plunging the weapon down. . .

"GOT HIM!" called Atalanta as, at the same instant, her arrow thudded into the horseman's heart. The scowl turned into a grimace of pain and he toppled to the ground.

Jason leaped back onto his feet, scrambled across the grass, snatched up the fleece and ran for the ship. Spears and arrows were flying over his head toward the mounted men. The Argonauts were on the attack. Zetes and Calais flew up and rained down arrows from above. Half a dozen soldiers plunged to the ground and lay sprawling on the riverbank. Then Periclymenus, the shape-shifter, changed into a lion and bounded out of the *Argo* into the middle of the remaining armed men. Their horses reared up in panic, threw their riders, turned tail and bolted into the depths of the forest.

Winded and stunned, the soldiers scrabbled around on the ground in total disarray, while Jason and the others climbed on board the ship. Lynceus untied the mooring rope, the rowers heaved on the oars, and the *Argo* shot off down the river and out of the reach of their enemies, with Jason standing proudly at the prow, holding the Golden Fleece triumphantly aloft.

. . . holding the Golden Fleece triumphantly aloft

Chapter eight

THE JOURNEY HOME

Jason's moment of triumph was short-lived. Seconds after the Argonauts' dramatic escape from the riverbank, King Aites himself sailed into the view around a bend in the river, standing on the prow of his warship, upstream of the *Argo*. Even at a distance, Jason could see that his body was rigid with fury and his face wore a murderous scowl – and he was getting closer by the minute.

"BRING BACK MY FLEECE!" he screamed. "BRING BACK MY FLEECE, YOU TREACHEROUS DOG!"

Jason leaped down to the rowing benches, furled the Golden Fleece at his feet and began to haul an oar through the turbid water. With Heracles beside him, they might have had some chance of outrowing Aites's hefty oarsmen, but now, badly outnumbered, there was nothing they could do to stop the king from catching up.

"Heave!" called Ancaeus desperately, but his urging made little difference. Aites's ship with its fearsome pointed bronze prow was gaining on them steadily. Soon it would crash into their stern, and

everything they had fought for would be lost. A hail of arrows, let loose by the king's archers, plopped into the water just short of the *Argo*. The archers were getting ready to fire again.

It was then that Medea took action. But what she did was so unspeakably brutal and barbarous, that even the most battle-hardened survivors of the Trojan War were sickened beyond belief.

The moment she first saw Jason, Medea had sworn to herself she would do *anything* for him, and now was her chance to prove her love. Nothing – *nothing* – mattered except to help him escape with the fleece, so that is why, standing at the stern of the *Argo*, in full sight of her father, she raised a gleaming knife to Apsyrtus's throat.

Aites, powerless to intervene, watched in total disbelief and horror.

"NO-OOOOO!" he shrieked. But Medea sliced through her brother's neck, as efficiently as if she were sacrificing a lamb. As soon as he was dead, and with all the calm detachment of a butcher carving up a carcass, she began to dismember his body, chopping off his limbs and slicing up his torso.

By the time the Argonauts had realized what was happening, it was already too late. Castor dropped his oar and rushed over to try to seize the knife, but she fended him off, lashing out with the weapon, eyes flashing savagely, like a lioness defending her kill. The others looked on helplessly. If they stopped rowing for even a second, the king would catch up.

But Medea's plan worked. When she had cut her brother up, she cast his body, piece by piece, into the river and Aites, shaking, screaming and weeping uncontrollably, had to order his oarsmen to slow his ship, so that he could retrieve the bloody fragments of his son from the water.

"Barbarous, loathsome witch!" he wailed. "Have you no heart? Foul, disgusting, abominable. . . animal! No daughter of mine would ever. . . *could* ever. . . Oh! my darling little boy. . . my. . ." His words dissolved into a fit of violent sobbing as Apsyrtus's head was fished out of the river.

The last time Medea ever saw her father, he was drenched in blood,

howling with grief and cradling his son's head in his arms as if it were a newborn baby.

And so, by means of this indescribably cruel act, the Argonauts made their escape from Colchis, back down the River Phasis and out into the Black Sea, with the Golden Fleece on board.

Now, for the first time since they had left the shores of Greece, the magic prow began to speak. And it was the voice of the goddess Hera that directed their homeward course.

If they returned by their outward route, Aites could easily follow, so Hera had devised another, partly by sea, partly along rivers, and partly overland where they had to carry or haul the ship for days on end, following the prow's meticulous directions – turn left – left again – now right – straight on.

Mile after mile they trudged, up hills and mountains, through bogs and across streams, until they reached the sea again.

With Hera's help they avoided many dangers, but there were still hardships to endure before they reached home. And getting home was now their sole aim – home to a triumphant heroes' welcome, to friends and family, to fortune and feasts, with Jason as king. .

But for the moment they were about to undergo one of the most hazardous ordeals known to sailors, an ordeal which only one man before them – the great hero Ulysses – had survived. And Hera was advising them how to face it:

"Just south of here is the island of the Sirens – a group of perilously jagged rocks which have been the cause of hundreds of shipwrecks. We must pass by them to get back to Greece."

Even the word "Sirens" instantly filled the crew with dread. As children they had been told about these monsters with beautiful female faces and enchanting voices who sang so bewitchingly that every passing sailor was drawn to his death on the rocks. They knew that the only way they could possibly survive was with the goddess's help, so they paid full attention as she spoke.

"When we get nearer to the island, Orpheus will begin to play his lyre and I will begin to sing. You must keep your eyes on the prow and listen to our song. You must listen to us and *only* us – remember your lives depend on it."

Her voice was unusually solemn and stern and the Argonauts listened carefully to every word, especially to her final warning which was issued in song. And as she sang, Orpheus began to play.

. . . singing the words of an eerily sweet and silvery song

"However sweet the Sirens' song,
However loud they sing,
Listen only to this music,
And Jason will be king.

If the Sirens' lure is greater,
Soon you'll meet your death,
In Poseidon's watery kingdom,
Drawing your last breath.

Sailors, you must heed my warning,
Listen to my song,
Stop your ears against the Sirens,
Or you'll drown ere long.

Listen to my singing, sailors,
Listen to my song,
Listen only to this music,
Or you'll drown ere long."

While Hera was singing, they all gradually became aware of another sound drifting in across the water. If they had allowed themselves to listen, they would have heard a song so sweet and melodious and so mysteriously enchanting that it was impossible not to be drawn to it, but the Argonauts kept their eyes firmly on the prow and their ears focused on Hera's song.

Orpheus played louder and louder as they approached the Sirens' island, and Hera repeated the final verse over and over again with an insistent beat. All of the Argonauts started singing with her and drumming on the rowing benches in time to the rhythm. All except one.

Butes, the youngest member of the crew, found his head turning to look at the island. And there he saw the loveliest faces he had ever seen – perfect olive skin and shining eyes and luscious lips singing the words of an eerily sweet and silvery song that floated in through his ears and worked its way around his brain. He had to listen. He *had* to listen. Somehow he must get nearer to them, drink in their music, envelop himself in their entrancing song, abandon himself to their magnetic charms.

In an instant he was mesmerized.

With the strength of a madman, he broke free of the hands that were pinning him to the bench. They were nothing to him, these strange people who only wanted to hold him back from what he knew he must have. He allowed his eyes to glaze over. He surrendered himself entirely to the trance, to the rapture of the beautiful music that whirled and danced around and around inside his head. Soon he would be with them – his angels. They were singing for him and him alone. He was in ecstasy. He found his legs were climbing over the edge of the ship. Hands were reaching out to pull him back, but he would not let them stop him. No one could stop him. Now he was free, jumping into the air, falling and falling down to the beautiful music, down to freedom. Down to. . .

Butes smashed into the rocks head-first, and the next wave washed his body out into the ocean. The dull thud of his fall momentarily drowned out the Sirens' song, but they did not stop singing, even for a second as the *Argo* drifted slowly past, and their eyes shone in delight when they saw tears of sorrow streaming down the cheeks of the ship's captain, who was still singing through gritted teeth.

Enormously saddened by Butes death, but relieved that no one else had succumbed to the Sirens' evil charms, the Argonauts sailed on. When they approached the island of Corsica, the *Argo* came to a sudden and inexplicable halt. A stiff breeze was filling the sail, the rowers were hauling on the oars, but the ship wouldn't budge an inch. Jason went up to the prow and demanded to know why.

"You have offended Zeus," was Hera's reply. "You are stained with the blood of an innocent child. You cannot go home until you are purified."

It was the first time Apsyrtus's murder had even been mentioned since their escape from Colchis. Everyone was still shocked and revolted by what had happened, but also knew that Medea's ruthless act had saved them from defeat and probably death.

"How do we go about that?" Jason asked. But the prow remained stubbornly silent.

Medea stepped forward. Her face was deathly pale and her hands were trembling. Though she had hardly said a word since she had killed her brother, not for one second had she been able to forget about it, because Zeus had sent the Furies to remind her. The Furies were spirits of vengeance with dogs' heads and bats' wings. They hounded murderers – especially those who had killed a relative – and they had been tormenting her relentlessly with horrible nightmares and awful daytime hallucinations.

"I have an idea," she said quietly.

"Do you?" said Jason, struggling hard with his own ambivalent feelings about her.

"My aunt, Circe, lives near here," said Medea, deliberately avoiding his gaze. "She is a much more powerful sorceress than I am. Maybe she could help us."

"We'll give it a try," said Jason with little enthusiasm, wishing that he had another choice.

They turned the ship around and began to sail back the way they had come. Hera's voice started up again, guiding them in to the island where Circe lived.

Jason and Medea left the crew moored in an inlet and set off to find Circe. Medea led the way through the trees, up a steep mountain path beside a stream. As they walked, she prepared Jason to meet her aunt.

"Whatever you do, don't get on the wrong side of her," she warned. "She has a very unpleasant habit of turning unwanted visitors into pigs. Be polite – but don't grovel." They were approaching a low stone cottage set partly into the mountainside. The herb garden in the front was inhabited by dozens of cats of all different sizes and markings.

"Thank the gods it's only cats now," Medea declared. "She used to keep lions and wolves!"

She suddenly grabbed hold of Jason's arm, stopping him in his tracks. The door of the cottage was opening.

"I almost forgot the most important part," she said in a insistent whisper. "Above all else, do *not* let her fall in love with you – the last time that happened, the poor man was stuck here for a year."

A tall, grey-haired figure wearing a long, blue robe and numerous strings of ceramic beads appeared in the doorway.

When they got closer, the figure sprinted up to them with outstretched arms, and Jason saw that she had the most astonishingly clear green eyes.

"Medea! *Darling!*" she said in a deep,

husky voice. "How *lovely* to see you. And is this your new man? Well, isn't he simply *gorgeous!*" With the words tumbling out in a torrent, she ran her hands appreciatively over Jason's leopard skin, then gave Medea an enormous bear hug and showered her with kisses.

"Do come in, darlings," she said, leading them over to her cottage. "I was expecting you – had a dream that you'd come. I was just having a goblet of my homemade wine. I know you'd love to join me."

"Thank you," said Jason.

The tiny low rooms of the cottage were packed from floor to rafters with an incredible jumble of things – papyrus scrolls, carved stone tablets, bottles, flasks, goblets, jars of paint, brushes, mirrors, seashells, feathers, branches, dried leaves and garlands of flowers, swathes of patterned material, bronze tools, vases and baskets, terracotta pots, silver lamps, gold trinkets, wooden chests, caskets, a huge bronze cauldron and countless cats. The parts of the walls that were visible were covered in murals, painted – Circe informed them – by her own hand.

"So, was my dream right?" she asked Medea, handing them their goblets of wine. "Did you really kill Apsyrtus?"

Medea nodded. Her eyes brimmed with tears and for the first time she allowed herself to give in to her grief, falling to her knees on the floor, sobbing uncontrollably and wailing out all her pain, anguish and remorse.

"Oh dear, oh dear," said Circe, bending down to put a sympathetic arm around her niece's shoulders. "The things we do when that reckless young Eros gets involved."

A little later, when Medea had recovered, Circe, clutching her magic wand and a bunch of herbs, led them out through the garden and up beside the mountain stream to a small natural pool, fed by a waterfall. They waded waist-high into the clear, bubbling water, and there, surrounded by trees, flowers, ferns and birdsong, Circe performed a cleansing ritual to wash away the horror of Apsyrtus's sacrifice, calling upon Zeus the Purifier to calm the anger of the Furies. From deep in the pool, a water nymph watched and smiled.

Circe lit a fire when they got back to her cottage, and cooked them a magical healing meal. When they had eaten as much as they could, they sat in front of the roaring blaze, with Circe dispensing wit, wisdom and homemade wine in equal measures, until an untroubled sleep overtook them all.

The *Argo* set sail the next morning, but the voyage from Circe's island back to Iolcus did not go entirely smoothly. Passing along the west coast of Greece, the ship was hit by a terrifying storm whipped up by Poseidon and Boreas and was blown completely off course. When they finally reached familiar waters again, after days of nonstop rowing and sailing across the Mediterranean, everyone was totally exhausted and starving. They decided to stop off at the island of Crete to rest and find food.

No sooner had they entered the port, than an enormous rock came crashing into the water at the *Argo's* stern, soaking the crew and flooding the deck. Jason looked up to where the rock had come from to see a massive metal giant, arms raised above its head, about to hurl another rock.

"It's Talos," said Medea quickly, "the guardian of this island – he belongs to King Minos. Hephaestus made him out of. . . UUUGH!" Another great wave washed over them. "Bronze," continued Medea through straggling strands of soaking wet hair. "Now get me to land. I have to distract him."

With rocks dropping all around, they rowed to the shore, where Medea leaped nimbly out of the ship and strode fearlessly up to the giant, holding out a cup of potion.

"Look what I've got for you," she said, as though talking to a baby. "If you drink this, you will live forever and ever,"

"But he'll live for ever, anyway," muttered Atalanta grumpily, back on the ship. "He's an automaton – a robot!"

"Shhhh!" said Jason. "I can't hear what she's saying."

"And it will make you so big and strong," coaxed Medea in a sing-song voice.

"But he's already big and strong!" scoffed Atalanta.

"Shut up, Atalanta," said Jason.

"Come on you handsome thing," Medea was saying, "Just one little sip – *please* – just for me."

Talos's metal joints creaked as he bent down to take the cup. He drained the potion in one noisy gulp, swayed, tottered on his enormous legs and then clattered to the ground. Medea ran over to one of his huge feet. At the back of his ankle was a metal stopper which she yanked out. A clear liquid began to trickle out of the hole and drip down the rocks.

While Talos slept, the liquid which gave him life slowly drained away. The Argonauts could land safely. Medea had saved them again.

After two days and nights on the island, the Argonauts were ready for the final leg of their homeward journey. With a mounting sense of excitement, they sailed through the myriad small islands of the Aegean Sea, up the length of Euboean coast and finally into the sheltered bay of Pagasae near Iolcus.

The sun was setting over Mount Pelion when they reached home waters. The Golden Fleece sparkled in Jason's hands. Standing proudly on the prow of his ship, he thought about all the adventures and dangers they had survived – the storms and the battles, the wrath of the gods, the monsters and giants. He thought about the Argonauts who hadn't made it home – Hylas and Idmon, the pilot Tiphys, and poor young Butes – and the courage and fortitude of those who had. He wondered where Heracles might be now.

Looking up to Pelion's peak, he remembered Chiron, the huge, kindly centaur who had brought him up. *"A long, long journey. . . a chance to wear a crown."* Those had been Chiron's words the night before he left the cave. It seemed like a lifetime ago he had walked down the mountain and carried that old woman across the stream. *"You won't regret it,"* she had said, in a voice that was. . . familiar! *Hera!* he realized suddenly. He had carried the goddess Hera across the stream! And she'd been as good as her word, directing their homeward journey and helping them through a multitude of dangers. He didn't know that Medea falling in love with him and aiding his escape with the fleece had also been part of Hera's plan, but he still offered a heartfelt prayer of thanks to the goddess for her assistance and guidance.

Surveying the city of Iolcus, with its terracotta rooftops glowing warmly in the sun's setting rays, he remembered how, as an eager, trusting and wide-eyed young man, he had marched boldly into Pelias's palace and accepted the king's challenge to bring back the Golden Fleece. And now here he was, sailing home holding the object of his quest in his hands, a boy no longer, but a hero coming home to claim his kingdom.

Chapter nine

THE HEROES' RETURN

An old fisherman was sitting on the beach mending his nets when a bright light far out at sea caught his eye. Throwing the nets to one side, and wincing at the pain in his stiff old joints, he got slowly to his feet, hobbled down to the water's edge and squinted out across the waves. Something in the distance was glittering in the evening sun.

Shielding his eyes from the harsh glare, the old man stood transfixed, peering intently at the dazzling shape as it floated slowly to the shore. Then he heard himself give a gasp of surprise. He had realized what he was looking at. The Golden Fleece! The famous Golden Fleece!

"Upon my soul," he said out loud when the ship was close enough for him to be able to see Jason's face. "But I thought that young man was. . ." His voice trailed off and he scratched his head quizzically.

The *Argo* drifted gently onto the sand and the crew jumped down into the shallow water. The beach was deserted, except for the old fisherman who was gazing at them with a puzzled frown.

"Good evening," said Jason to the old man.

"Good evening, sir," he replied.

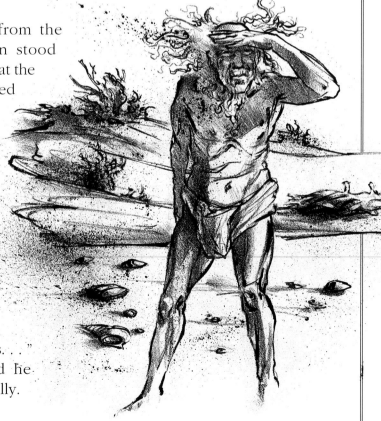

"I wonder if I might be so bold as to ask, sir," he ventured, "if you are that young Jason – the one who set off to get the Golden Fleece from Colchis?"

"One and the same," said Jason with a broad smile, flourishing the fleece proudly.

"But everyone said you were – how can I put this? You've been gone such a long time, you see, they all gave you up for. . . dead!"

"Did they indeed!" said Jason with a laugh. "Well, they're going to be in for a shock, aren't they?"

"But you don't understand, sir," said the fisherman anxiously. "When he heard that you were dead and that his own son Acastus had died in the shipwreck too, that King Pelias did some dreadful things – I mean *really* dreadful things – I don't rightly know if I can tell you about them, sir."

As the old man spoke, Jason's sense of elation began to evaporate, along with the imagined scenes of joyful reunion and celebration that he had pictured in his head all the way back from Colchis. The old man's worried expression was making him nervous.

"What in the name of Zeus are you talking about, man?" he snapped. The Golden Fleece suddenly felt very heavy in his hands. He lowered his arms, relaxed his hold and let it slide down his legs onto the sand.

"A few months after you had left, sir," the old man continued diffidently, staring at the ground, "King Pelias let old King Aeson – let your father – out of prison. A while later your mother had. . ." His voice began to waver and his rheumy old eyes filled with tears.

"Had what?" said Jason, grabbing the man roughly by the shoulders, as if to shake the story out of him.

"Had a baby, sir – a baby boy – Promachus they called him."

Jason grinned with relief and released his grip, but then, registering the sadness in the old man's face, remembered, like a punch in the stomach, the vow that Pelias had made – the vow to kill all of Aeson's children. His fleeting moment of happiness was instantly transformed into a sickening sense of foreboding.

"And?" Jason prompted.

"Well, Pelias found out about the baby. He snatched the poor little thing from your mother. . ." His voice faded.

"Yes?" said Jason quietly.

"Sir, I really don't know how to tell you this."

"JUST SAY IT!"

"He dashed out its brains on the palace floor."

Jason's face turned white. A wave of nausea swept through him and his knees went weak. It was as much as he could do not to collapse to the ground. Then came a sharp gust of grief, followed by a sweeping backwash of anger.

But there was worse to come. He

could see it in the old man's downcast eyes and in the awkward way he held himself as he spoke.

"They say your mother was so distraught that she. . ." He paused again, then tried another tack. "She thought she'd lost two sons, you see. She was inconsolable, so—" He gulped loudly before quickly spluttering, "she killed herself. And as for your father. . ."

"What happened to my father?" whispered Jason through clenched teeth.

"Your father drank poison, and died."

This time Jason let the feelings flood in and overwhelm him. He sank down onto the Golden Fleece, buried his face in the thick wool and howled.

The old man, exhausted by the

"PELIAS SHALL PAY!" he roared

task he had found himself having to perform, lowered himself slowly to his knees and placed his skinny hand on Jason's back in a token gesture of comfort. There was nothing else he could do.

In a whirlwind of emotion, Jason suddenly realized what a stupid, gullible fool he had been. Pelias had lied. He never had any intention of handing over the kingdom. He had just wanted to get rid of him. He had sent him halfway across the world in the hope he would never return. All the hardship and suffering, all the dangers and adventures of the past few months meant nothing now. His mother was dead. His father was dead. And the baby brother he had never even seen was dead.

Snatching handfuls of wool with flailing arms, he tore at the fleece frantically, trying to rip it to bits. So much sorrow. So much pain – and for what? This worthless *thing*. It couldn't bring back his family. It meant nothing. The Argonauts watched helplessly, some shedding tears of sympathy for their leader, now a pathetic sight, lying face down on the fleece, racked with harrowing sobs and thrashing his arms around. But as they watched, a change came over him. The shaking subsided. The tears stopped, and when he finally rolled over, his face was set in a savage, resolute snarl. Fury at his betrayal had overcome his sorrow. He pulled himself up onto his

knees and raised his tear-stained face to the darkening sky.

"PELIAS SHALL PAY!" he roared, easily drowning out the sound of the breaking waves and the cries of the wheeling gulls.

"PELIAS SHALL PAY! SO HELP ME ZEUS!"

Jason's mind was made up. Only one thing would satisfy him now.

Revenge.

Jason was all for storming into Iolcus and slaughtering Pelias on the spot, but the palace was well guarded and they were ill equipped to launch such an attack. And Acastus pointed out that he could hardly be expected to help kill his own father.

It was Medea who came up with a plan. First she made the old fisherman swear to keep their return a secret, then she asked the Argonauts to hide the ship and themselves in a wood behind a beach within sight of Iolcus. She said she was going to the city and when they saw torches burning on the palace roof, it would mean that her plan had been successful and the city was theirs for the taking.

It took Medea all the next day to make her preparations. She left the ship at dawn, and by nightfall was approaching the city disguised as an elderly woman, leading a bleary-eyed old ram and pulling a cart on which there sat a statue of the goddess Artemis and a large bronze cauldron on a stand.

"Make way! Make way for the goddess," she called to the guards at the city gates. "Message for the king from the goddess Artemis! Good fortune to all citizens!" The startled guards did not dare disobey. Artemis was the daughter of Zeus and a quick-tempered, volatile goddess. Anyone who offended her always paid a severe penalty.

By the light of a full moon, Medea made her way through the streets of Iolcus, across the marketplace and past the temple to the palace, calling out her message in a loud, shrill voice as she went. Pelias, awakened by her cries, was ready to meet her when she reached the gates.

"What's all this about?" he asked, accompanying her into the palace, where his three grown-up daughters, also roused from sleep, were waiting in the great hall to find out what was happening.

"Artemis wants to reward you for your devotion to her," said Medea in a croaking old woman's voice. "She wants to make you young again so you can father another son and heir – she heard about the tragic loss of your son with those foolhardy Argonauts."

"And why on earth should I believe that you have come from Artemis, old woman?" said Pelias scornfully, stepping across the room to sit down on a couch.

"Because she did the same for me!" said Medea, suddenly spinning around and around on the spot, so that her cloak swirled out in a circle. When she came to a standstill, she had magically transformed herself back into a young woman.

Pelias was clearly impressed.

"Such is the power of the great goddess Artemis!" declared Medea emphatically. "And she can transform you too."

"What do I have to do?" asked Pelias eagerly.

"I'll show you."

She reached under the folds of her cloak and, with a flourish, produced a curved, gleaming knife. The old ram which had been waiting patiently, tied to the cart, uttered a feeble bleat of protest as Medea dragged it to her.

"Bring me some water!" she called theatrically to the slaves. "Make me a fire!" Pelias nodded his assent.

While the slaves scuttled to and fro with sticks and pitchers, building a fire under the cauldron and filling it up with water, Medea, like a conjuror performing her most famous trick, slaughtered the old ram and cut it into thirteen pieces.

"Thirteen – the magic number!" she proclaimed, throwing the last pieces of bloody meat into the

cauldron, where the water was beginning to bubble. "Beloved by goddesses and sorceresses alike – and now the magic words."

An aroma of boiling meat began to pervade the hall as Medea chanted over the cauldron, waving her hands around in dramatic gestures, grabbing at the edge of her cloak to make it billow around her, then stretching up her arms as though invoking the goddess Artemis.

Pelias seemed mesmerized by her performance. "Now watch carefully!" Medea ordered.

She leaned over the cart, holding out her cloak so that momentarily it partially enveloped both the cauldron and the statue, then reached down through the steam into the cauldron and produced a frisky young lamb which she held triumphantly aloft.

The onlookers clapped and cheered, all utterly convinced that they had witnessed the rejuvenation of the old ram. In the midst of her theatrics, no one had seen her reach inside the hollow statue to grab the concealed lamb, before appearing to pluck it from the cauldron, like a rabbit from a hat.

"And now, with your help, I will rejuvenate your father," said Medea, turning to Pelias's daughters.

"Replenish the fire and the water," she commanded the slaves, before stepping over to the couch. Pelias did not hesitate for even a second and eagerly complied with her requests that he should lie down, close his eyes and relax. A pungent perfume filled his nostrils when Medea removed the stopper from the small bottle she had taken from under her cloak. He felt the cold drops of sleeping potion on his eyelids, heard Medea's soft voice telling him that when he woke up he would be young and handsome again; all the pain and stiffness in his joints would be gone; all the wrinkles in his leathery old skin smoothed away and all his wiry grey hair replaced by the glossy black locks of his youth. Then he fell asleep.

"Thirteen pieces," Medea said to Evadne, Pelias's eldest daughter, holding out the knife, handle first. "The magic number."

Evadne looked to her sisters. The youngest, Alcestis, was staring at her feet. Amphinome, the middle one, was looking worried.

"The goddess Artemis does not show mercy to those who disobey her," said Medea quietly.

Evadne reached out and took the knife.

"Remember, he feels nothing," said Medea, moving back over to the couch. She lifted one of Pelias's arms by the wrist and then let it fall. It flopped down lifelessly on his leg with a loud slap. Evadne walked over to the couch.

"The sooner you do it, the sooner he'll be young again," said Medea in gentle, comforting tones. "If you love your father, you will do as I tell you. It is the will of Artemis."

Evadne took a deep breath, raised the knife and plunged it straight into her father's stomach. Alcestis gave a little groan and turned her head away, but Amphinome called to the slaves for another knife and came over to help her sister.

Between them they dissected their father's body into thirteen pieces and dropped them one by one into the cauldron. Alcestis could not bring herself to take part, but she did not try to stop them, believing, like everyone else in the room, that soon her father would appear before them, miraculously transformed, full of the strength and vitality of youth, rising phoenix-like from the bubbling stew of human meat.

"For human rejuvenation, there is another part of the ritual that must be performed." said Medea, when Evadne had tossed the last piece of her father – his head – into the cauldron. "While we wait for it to boil, we must go to the roof and invoke great Artemis, goddess of the moon. Grab a burning torch and follow me."

Pelias's daughters did as Medea commanded. While she led them in a solemn, torch-lit procession up to the palace roof, the slaves and guards, who, intrigued by the sounds of Medea's performance, had deserted their posts and come in to watch, gathered around the cauldron, peering intently through the steam at Pelias's grizzled head rolling around in the greasy grey mixture, waiting for him to rise up rejuvenated from the seething stew. Waiting in vain.

Down below on the beach, the Argonauts saw the distant gleam of torches up on the palace roof. It was the signal they had been waiting for. They grabbed their weapons and rushed into Iolcus, taking the city by storm. They met little opposition at the gates or when they rampaged into the palace, where they came across a pathetic scene. Pelias's daughters had just realized that they had been tricked into killing their own father, and now they stood around the cauldron which contained his congealing remains, weeping and bemoaning Medea's treachery.

Even the sight of their brother Acastus, whom they had all believed to be dead, did little to assuage their grief and guilt. The guards had all left to spread the news of Pelias's strange demise. Medea was nowhere to be seen.

It was against this backdrop and accompanied by the sound of the sisters' wailing that Jason finally took possession of the throne of Iolcus. As he stepped up onto the podium, he thought again about the last time he had been in the palace, as an eager young man with a taste for adventure and a burning passion to avenge the wrongs that Pelias had done his father.

He did feel sympathy for Pelias's daughters – and for Acastus, whom he had come to like and respect over the many months they had spent at sea. It wasn't their fault that they had such an evil tyrant for a father. But he knew he had done the right thing.

Sitting awkwardly on the uncomfortable throne, he let his eyes wander across the vast expanse of the marble floor, imagining the scene when Pelias has snatched his baby brother from his mother's arms. He wondered exactly where the poor tiny mite had met his barbaric death.

Jason sensed his heart harden. All he could feel was hatred for the dead man who had betrayed him so cruelly and treated his family so mercilessly – hatred tinged with the harsh comfort of revenge.

Chapter ten

MEDEA'S REVENGE

If only there could have been a happy ending! If only the Argonauts could have had a glorious homecoming, a triumphal procession through the streets of Iolcus and a grand celebration of their success.

But that is not what happened.

Instead, there was a horrified reaction to the cruel way in which Medea had disposed of Pelias, and a solemn vow from Acastus to avenge his father's death.

"I am bound by family duty to seek revenge," he told his sisters dispassionately, but even in their own anguish, they could detect the still greater depth of sorrow in his eyes as he resolved to oppose his old comrade.

Acastus and his sisters fled from the palace and soon drummed up the support of Pelias's followers, along with many others in the town who did not want to accept Jason as king.

Within hours, an angry armed mob was surrounding the palace, demanding that Jason should surrender the throne.

"How quickly they forget," he said sadly when he heard the commotion. But this was no time for regrets. The mob was beating on the gates, threatening to storm the palace, and the Argonauts, barricaded inside the throne room, were badly outnumbered.

There was only one thing to do: flee for their lives. But how? They could hardly fight their way out through hundreds of furious citizens who were brandishing flaming torches and beating swords on shields.

The answer came in the form of an ancient serving woman who had stood on the sidelines when Medea was performing her deadly act, and had remained a silent witness when Jason took possession of the throne.

Now the hunched little figure, shrouded in black, stepped forward, raised her time-battered face to the Argonaut and spoke softly.

"You were in danger in this palace once before, young man," she said. "And I rescued you."

Jason registered his surprise. He was certain he had never laid eyes on the woman before.

"Of course it was a very long time

ago," she went on, "and you were much too tiny to know what was going on. You were bawling your head off at the time!"

Atalanta laughed. Jason glared at her and moved closer to the old woman. Her rasping voice was now barely audible over the sound of the baying crowd outside the gates.

"I attended your mother at your birth, you see," confided the woman, "and hardly had the cord been cut when she thrust you into my arms and begged me to take you far away from the palace – up into the mountains – to Chiron's cave."

"Your mother told me about a secret underground tunnel that leads from the palace to outside the city gates. And that's how I smuggled you out, clutching you tightly in my arms" – she mimed the action – "I fought my way through spiders' webs to the outside world. You yelled and yelled."

Suddenly she flinched at a tremendously loud crash from the courtyard.

"They've broken down the gates!" said Lynceus. He was squinting through a tiny crack between the big wooden doors. "They're heading this way!"

Shaken at last from her reminiscence, the old lady got to the point of her story. "It still exists, as far as I know – the tunnel," she gabbled. "It's your only means of escape."

Jason didn't know whether to thank the old lady or ask her what in Zeus's name this had to do with the situation they now faced. In fact he did neither, because she was determined to continue without interruption.

"How can we trust you?" Jason asked.

"Jason!" shouted Medea in exasperation. "We haven't got time for that. We have to trust her!" She rushed over to the woman.

"Show us, please show us," she implored. "We have to leave now!" The babble of voices reached an angry crescendo at the throne room door. Wood splintered as an axe head came crashing through.

"Hurry – *please!*" urged Jason.

The old woman gathered up her long skirt and hobbled as fast as she could across the room to a small door in the corner. She tugged it open to reveal a narrow flight of steps leading down into the gloom.

"Down as far as you can to the storeroom," she said hurriedly. "There's a row of huge storage jars. Find the one with the serpent mark. Slide the jar back. Lift the flagstone underneath. That's the entrance. Now go!"

Jason was already leaping down the steps, closely followed by the others.

"Last one replace the flagstone!" called the old lady. "Good luck!" she added as she slammed the door after them.

"MURDERER!" Acastus screamed a fraction of a second later, bursting into the room at swordpoint. But all that confronted him was an ancient, hunched old lady, dressed in black, with a faint smile on her lips.

Acastus and his mob tore around the palace searching for the Argonauts

and shouting at the tops of their voices. By the time they reached the storeroom, Jason was well on his way to safety, through the dark, dusty tunnel.

In the chaos and confusion above, no one noticed a storage jar out of place, a spilled flask of oil and a few floury footprints on the worn flagstones.

Once outside the city, the Argonauts instinctively made their way back to the *Argo*, but there seemed to be no reason for them to remain together any more. Sadly and reluctantly, the crew began to disperse, making their way back to their home towns or setting off in search of new adventures.

Zetes and Calais flew off through the morning mist. Castor and Polydeuces wandered off along the shore. Orpheus retrieved his lyre from its hiding place, said a tearful goodbye to Jason and Medea and followed after the twins.

"It was fun," said Atalanta with a far from fun-filled expression on her face. Even Atalanta, the great and fearless warrior, looked like she was about to burst into tears.

"But I'm sure there are plenty more adventures in the world," she added with a gulp. "I'm off to look for Heracles."

"Good luck, Atalanta," said

Medea, hugging her.

"Thanks," was all that Jason could manage.

They watched her bound off along the shore.

🏛🏛🏛🏛🏛🏛🏛🏛🏛🏛🏛🏛🏛

Jason and Medea sailed the *Argo* to Orchomenos in Boeotia – where all those years before, Princess Helle and Prince Phrixus had been rescued by the Golden Ram sent by Zeus. There they went straight to Zeus's temple and hung the Golden Fleece among the statues and other treasures for all to see.

Then they set sail for Corinth where, with the help of some local fishermen, they hauled the *Argo* up onto the shore and dedicated it to Poseidon.

Finally Jason fulfilled the promise he had made to Medea months before among the jars, potions, herbs and cauldrons of her boudoir in Colchis. He married her.

They decided to settle in Corinth. Medea had spent her childhood in that city because her father, King Aites, had been its ruler before he emigrated to Colchis. The man whom Aites had appointed to rule in his absence died soon after Jason and Medea arrived, leaving no heirs. As King Aites's daughter, Medea had a claim to the throne, and the people were happy to accept her as their queen and Jason as their king.

And so, at last, Jason had the "chance to wear a crown" that Chiron had foreseen so many years before. It was not the crown that he had undergone so many dangers for, but that hardly seemed to matter now. Jason was king, and despite the lack of celebration at their homecoming, tales of Jason and the Argonauts and their heroic adventures began to spread around Greece and then further afield. Jason was a hero.

If only it could be said that King Jason and Queen Medea lived happily ever after, had a long and glorious reign, lived together peacefully until a ripe old age, ruled their people wisely, won everyone's respect and admiration and watched their children and grandchildren grow up.

But that is not what happened.

For a while they were happy enough, however, especially when Medea gave birth to twin

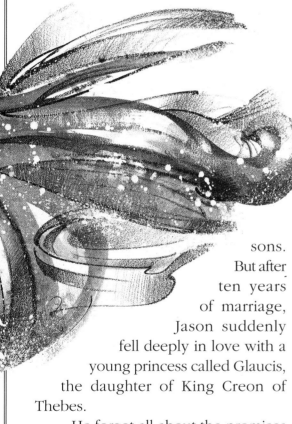

sons. But after ten years of marriage, Jason suddenly fell deeply in love with a young princess called Glaucis, the daughter of King Creon of Thebes.

He forgot all about the promises he had made to Medea when she saved his life in Colchis. He forgot all about how many times she had helped the Argonauts. He forgot all about the vows he'd made to her on their wedding day and he forgot that she was his faithful wife and the mother

of his sons. He wanted her out of his life. He wanted a divorce.

Medea was furious. Medea was consumed with jealousy and hatred. She was still as head-over-heels in love with Jason as at the moment when Eros's little love arrow had pierced her heart.

After everything she'd done for him, how could he just discard her like an old boot? Banish her from the palace? – *her* palace! It was unbelievable! Outrageous! Despicable!

Medea was furious, but Medea was also clever. She wasn't just going to submit to the rejection.

Medea hatched a plan.

She pretended that she was not angry, bitter or jealous and accepted the divorce without fuss. She even smiled at Glaucis when she came to visit. She smiled even more sweetly as she persuaded Jason to allow her to remain in the palace for just one more day while she prepared her things to leave. Instead she prepared her revenge.

Jason and Glaucis were in the throne room discussing their wedding arrangements when one of Jason's sons came in carrying a large bundle.

"What have you got there, lad?" asked Jason.

"A wedding present for Glaucis – from mother," replied the boy.

"How kind!" exclaimed Glaucis, rushing over to grab the bundle.

"You should wait till we're married!" joked Jason, but the princess was already tearing open the wrappings.

"Oh!" she squealed. "They're lovely!"

She held out a beautifully woven robe and golden crown for Jason to admire.

"Very beautiful," he observed. "You should try them on."

Glaucis eased the crown onto her pretty head. It was a perfect fit. Less cautiously, she thrust her hands into the arms of the robe and wrapped its rich folds around her, luxuriating in its soft warmth.

"Isn't it simply gorgeous!" she enthused, twirling around the room. "Isn't it just— AAAAAAAAH!" her face suddenly contorted into a mask of agony and incomprehension. Her hands began to snatch desperately at the crown, trying to tear it from her head.

"What is it?" yelled Jason. "What's happening?"

Glaucis could only scream in reply and scrabble frantically at the robe, trying to wrench it off. But the fabric was stuck fast to her skin and the crown was fixed tight on her head, and the poisons with which Medea had impregnated them were burning into her flesh.

Jason leaped down from the throne to help her, but was thrown back by a sudden blast of heat. The robe had burst into flames! Soon Glaucis was a raging inferno, staggering around the room screaming and setting alight wall hangings and furniture. When finally she dropped to the floor, the flames engulfed her totally.

No one had heard, above the noise of her terrified screams, a distant, delighted cackle.

Medea had wreaked her revenge.

Within seconds the throne room was ablaze. Glaucis's father came running in to see what all the noise was about, but was met by a wall of flames. He didn't stand a chance. Servants were running around in a frenzy, screaming and shouting for water to quench the flames, but the fire was already out of control, raging through the sun-baked palace at a tremendous speed, consuming everything in its path – wooden chests, beds and blankets, roofs and staircases, floors, clothes, tapestries, furniture – and people.

Here there was no secret escape route for Jason, no wizened old lady to come to his rescue, and no magic potion to protect him against the searing heat of the inferno. Choking on the thick black smoke, he backed into a corner, holding his hands in front of his face against the fierce heat of the encroaching flames.

"Great Athene, help me!" he wailed. "Mighty Zeus have mercy!" He was flattened against the wall now. The flames were licking his feet. "Great goddess Hera, hear my prayer!"

His fingernails dug into the wall.

Medea's Revenge

Up on Mount Olympus Hera gave a weary sigh. She wasn't all that sure she could be bothered. He'd behaved like a pig to that poor Medea, after all. Some people were just never satisfied! Then she remembered how bravely he'd carried her across the river, how grateful and respectful he'd always been towards her.

"Oh all right!" she said begrudgingly. "I hear you."

Jason couldn't breathe. The acrid black smoke filled his eyes, his nose, his mouth, his lungs. He was blind and helpless. The heat was unbearable. His toes were burning. His arms were flailing up and down the wall in agony. He tossed his head from side to side but there was no refuge from the scorching heat on his skin.

He eased himself along the wall. His head was spinning. Any second he would drift into unconsciousness, sink down into the hellish void, be swallowed by the flames. His fingertips explored the wall – it was almost too hot to touch – and suddenly, like a miracle, felt an opening, a hole, a window! It didn't matter that he'd never seen it before. He didn't need to know where it had come from. It was his salvation, his lifeline, his escape route.

"Thank you Hera, thank you Hera, thank you," he gasped over and over again as he hauled himself out of the path of the crackling tongues of fire and up into the narrow opening. He eased himself through and plopped out onto the ground, wailing like something new-born as his burned feet hit the earth.

Barely conscious, he dragged himself away from the palace, wheezing and spluttering and gulping in great lungfuls of air. Just at that moment there was a huge explosion behind him. He rolled over onto his back in time to see Medea rising up out of the conflagration in a shining golden chariot drawn by two flying dragons. She laughed a maniacal laugh as she soared up through the smoke, up through the swirling heat haze and disappeared into the clouds.

Far below her the half-dead body of the man she still loved lay spread-eagled on the blackened earth, exhausted by his ordeal and gulping for breath like a fish out of water.

So what became of Medea, after she had fled the burning palace? Some say that she flew to Thebes, found Heracles and asked him to shelter her, but the Thebans would not let her stay in the city as soon as they found out that she had been responsible for the death of Creon, their king. After that it is said she went to Athens and married King Aegeus, but was soon after banished from that city for attempting to poison his son Theseus.

She laughed a maniacal laugh . . .

. . . as she soared up through the smoke

The truth is that Medea never really found happiness again. Try as she might, she could never forgive Jason for his betrayal. She became ever more twisted and vengeful, but until the very day she died, she swore that she still loved him.

And Jason? Jason crawled from the wreckage of the palace a broken man. In time the terrible burns on his feet healed, but he could never walk again without pain, and the scars never left him. Although Hera had come to his rescue one last time, from the moment he betrayed Medea he had lost the goodwill of the gods.

It is said that after the great fire, he picked over the remains of the palace day after day, frantically sifting the ashes and searching through the charred relics for a single trace of his beloved children, but none could be found. He hobbled off mournfully into the night and spent the rest of his days wandering homeless and alone from city to city.

Finally, in his old age, he came once more to Corinth and wandered through the crowded streets. He hardly recognized the place now, and no one knew who he was. But there, when he hobbled down to the beach, rotting slowly to pieces on the shore, just where they had left it, sat the *Argo*.

Jason limped over and eased himself down onto the sand in the shadow of the ship's great prow. He looked at his gnarled, scarred old feet and then raised his eyes to stare out at the shimmering sea, trying to picture the *Argo* in the old days, racing across the sparkling waves with her sail billowing out proudly in the sunlight, with Lynceus at the prow and Tiphys at the helm.

He craned his neck to look back at the rotting carcass of the ship. There was almost nothing left of the sail now, just a few scraps of ragged, sun-bleached linen, hanging on by a thread.

He settled himself onto his back and closed his eyes. As he drifted to sleep, faces from the past began to appear – the smiling warrior queen of Lemnos, Atalanta scowling as she demanded to set sail, Heracles's tear-stained cheeks when he stood on the shore crying "Hylas, Hylas," over and over again, King Cyzicus in his lion skin welcoming them to his wedding feast with open arms, blind King Phineus railing at the Harpies, Circe on her magical island – and there was Medea, beautiful, bewitching Medea, standing waist deep in a mountain pool fed by a waterfall.

Her face was suddenly blotted out by the vision of a huge dragon, lunging at him, teeth bared, then came the fire-breathing bulls snorting out great tongues of flame over his burning feet. Behind them, the Clashing Rocks smashed together with a thunderous roar and high above the Stymphalian birds and the screeching Harpies soared up and up into a cloudless sky.

"Fame and glory. . . a long, long journey. . . pain and tragedy. . . and a chance to wear a crown." It was Chiron's voice he imagined in his ear, whispering softly, like waves breaking gently on the shore. *"Fame and glory, fame and glory, fame and . . ."*

Jason was drifting through dreams when somewhere above him was a loud creak. He did not hear the prow – Athene's gift from her father's sacred oak tree at Dodona – crack. He did not see it fall. Nor did he feel the impact of the heavy lump of wood that crushed his skull and killed him. He was floating among monsters and memories when the great god Pluto sent Hermes flying into his dream to lead him gently out of this world and down into Pluto's kingdom. And there, in the Underworld, on the far side of the River Styx stood his two little boys, smiling and waving, ready to welcome him with open arms.

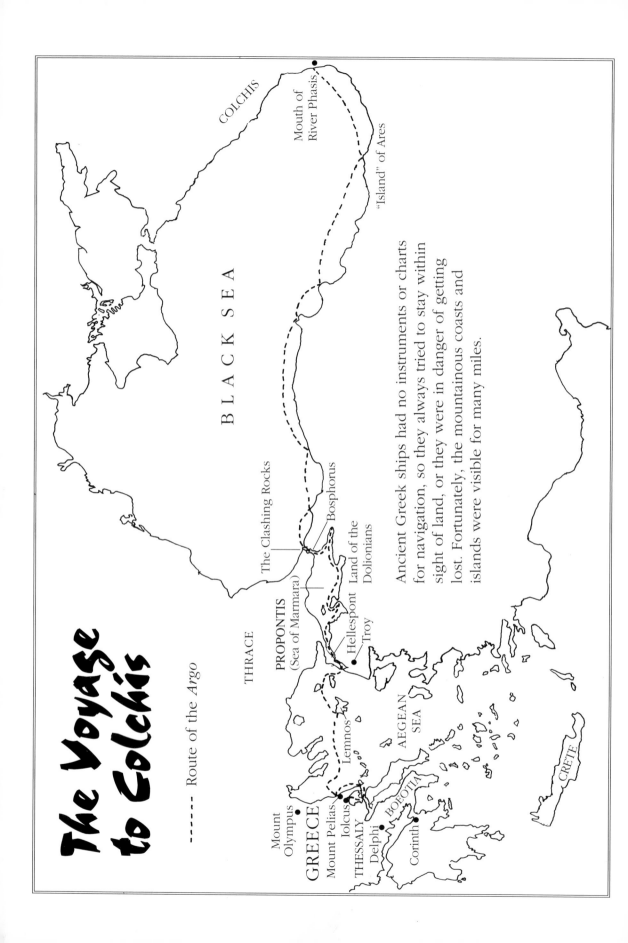

The Voyage to Colchis

----- Route of the Argo

COLCHIS

Mouth of River Phasis

"Island" of Ares

BLACK SEA

The Clashing Rocks

Bosphorus

PROPONTIS
(Sea of Marmara)

Land of the Dolionians

THRACE

Hellespont
Troy

Ancient Greek ships had no instruments or charts for navigation, so they always tried to stay within sight of land, or they were in danger of getting lost. Fortunately, the mountainous coasts and islands were visible for many miles.

AEGEAN SEA

Lemnos

Mount Olympus

GREECE

Mount Pelias
Iolcus

THESSALY
Delphi

BOEOTIA

Corinth

CRETE

WHO'S WHO

Acastus (ack-*ass*-tus) Son of King Pelias. With his sisters, Evadne, Alcestis and Amphinome, he opposes Jason after the death of Pelias.

Achilles (a-*kill*-ees) Greek hero of the Trojan War, raised by Chiron, the centaur.

Aegeus (ij-*ee*-us) 1. King Aites's youngest grandson, son of Phrixus and Chalciope. 2. King of Athens whom Medea marries after she escapes from Corinth. He banishes her from the city after she tries to poison his son, Theseus.

Aeolus (ee-*ole*-us) God. Ruler of the winds.

Aeson (*ee*-son) Jason's father, and rightful King of Iolcus, deposed by his half-brother Pelias. Husband of Polymele. Kills himself by drinking poison after his wife's death and the murder of his baby son.

King Aites (aye-*ee*-teez) King of Colchis and guardian of the Golden Fleece. Father of Medea, Chalciope and Apsyrtus. Sets Jason the "impossible" task of harnessing the Bulls of Ares and sowing the Field of Ares with dragon's teeth.

Alcestis (*al*-kess-tiss) Youngest daughter of King Pelias, and sister of Acastus.

Amazons (*am*-a-zonz) A race of fierce female warriors.

Amphinome (am-fin-*o*-me) Middle daughter of King Pelias, sister of Acastus.

King Amycus (*am*-i-kus) The boxing king of the Island of Bebrycos. Killed by Polydeuces in a boxing match.

Ancaeus (an-*ki*-us) Argonaut chosen as the new pilot after death of Tiphys.

Aphrodite (aff-ro-*die*-tee) Goddess of beauty and love, mother of Eros.

Apollo (a-*poll*-o) Sun god in charge of the sun's movements across the sky, also associated with music, archery, care of flocks, and prophecy. Son of Zeus, brother of Artemis.

Apsyrtus (*ap*-seer-tus) King Aites's son and brother of Medea and Chalciope. Brutally sacrificed by Medea to help the Argonauts escape from Colchis.

Argonauts (*are*-go-norts) The crew of the *Argo* (*are*-go) – the ship that Jason has built for the voyage to Colchis to get the Golden Fleece. There are 53 in total.

Argus (*are*-gus) Actor and craftsman who builds the *Argo*.

Artemis (*are*-tem-iss) Fiercely independent moon goddess and virgin huntress, in charge of the movement of the moon across the sky. Sister of Apollo, daughter of Zeus.

Atalanta (at-al-*an*-ta) The only female Argonaut and a renowned archer and runner. Was brought up by a bear when left out to die by her father and became a survival expert. She helps defeat the six-armed giants and the Stymphalian birds.

King Athamas (ath-*a*-mass) King of Orchomenos in Boeotia in Greece. Husband first of Nephele and then Ino. Father of Helle and Phrixus. Nearly sacrifices children to Zeus after being tricked by Ino.

Athene (a-*thee*-nee) Goddess of wisdom and war. Helps build the *Argo* and watches over the Argonauts during their quest. Daughter of Zeus, stepdaughter of Hera.

Boreas (*bore*-ee-ass) The North Wind, father of Zetes and Calais.

Butes (byoot-*aze*) The youngest Argonaut, lured to his death by the Sirens.

Cadmus (*cad*-muss) Phoenician prince and founder of the city of Thebes. He was advised by Athene to plant dragon's teeth from which grew armed warriors. Medea gives Jason some of the leftover teeth.

Calais (kall-*a*-iss) (see **Zetes**)

Castor and Polydeuces (*cass*-tor and polly-*dyoo*-seez) Argonauts. Twin sons of Zeus. Polydeuces is a champion boxer, Castor a wrestler. Polydeuces fights and kills King Amycus in a boxing match.

Princess Chalciope (kal-*see*-o-pee) Daughter of King Aites, sister of Medea, wife of Phrixus and mother of four men rescued by the Argonauts.

Chiron (*khee*-ron) A centaur (half man and half horse), renowned for his wisdom and kindness. He raised Jason and other Greek heroes in a cave on Mount Pelion.

Circe (*sir*-see) A powerful sorceress, sister of King Aites, aunt of Medea.

Princess Cleite (*kli*-tee) Wife of King Cyzicus. Kills herself when she hears her husband has been killed.

King Creon (*kree*-on) King of Thebes and father of Princess Glaucis. Killed in the fire at the royal palace at Corinth.

King Cyzicus (*key*-zee-kuss) King of the Dolionians, husband of Princess Cleite. Accidentally killed by Jason.

Demeter (de-*meet*-a) Goddess of the earth and harvests, responsible for growth of fruits and crops. Sister of Zeus, Hera and Poseidon.

Demigod/goddess Son/daughter of a god and a mortal.

Echion (*ekh*-ee-on) Son of Hermes, grandson of Zeus and the Argonauts' messenger and herald.

Eros (*ear*-oss) God of love. Son of Aphrodite. Specializes in making people fall in love. Fires arrow that makes Medea fall in love with Jason.

Evadne (ev-*ad*-nee) Eldest daughter of King Pelias, sister of Acastus.

The **Furies** (*fyoor*-eez) Demigoddesses with dogs' heads, snakes for hair and bats' wings. They inflict mental torment on murderers – especially those who have killed a relative.

Ganymede (*gan*-ee-meed) Friend of Eros. He started life as a mortal, but became immortal after Zeus took him to Mount Olympus to be a cup bearer to the gods. Very handsome.

Princess Glaucis (*glaw*-siss) Daughter of King Creon. Jason falls in love with her while still married to Medea. Killed by Medea.

The **Harpies** (*har*-pees) Winged monsters with female heads and screeching voices. Sent by Helios to plague King Phineus by snatching and ruining his food. Chased away by Zetes and Calais.

Helios (*hee*-lee-oss) God who drives the chariot of the sun across the sky each day. He inflicted the Harpies on King Phineus when, in exchange for a long life, the King chose to be blind.

Princess Helle (*hell*-a) Daughter of Nephele and King Athamas. Stepdaughter of Ino and sister of Phrixus. The Hellespont is named after her.

Hephaestus (heff-*eest*-us) Blacksmith of the gods. Made the Bulls of Ares and Talos, the robotic giant. Son of Hera, husband of Aphrodite.

Hera (*hair*-a) Queen of the gods. To test Jason, she disguises herself as an old woman and asks him to carry her across a swollen river. He passes this test and Hera then helps him during the quest for the Golden Fleece. Wife and sister of Zeus. Stepmother of Athene.

Heracles (*hair*-a-kleez) Argonaut. Son of Zeus. Strongest man in the world and very brave. Leaves the quest to look for his servant, Hylas, after he disappears.

Hermes (*her*-meez) Messenger of the gods. Son of Zeus. At the request of his uncle, Pluto, he leads dying people down into the Underworld. He brings the golden ram to rescue Helle and Phrixus when they are about to be sacrificed by their father, and leads Jason into the Underworld after his death.

Hylas (*hee*-las) Argonaut. Heracles's servant. He disappears when a water nymph falls in love with him and drags him down into her pool.

Queen Hypsipyle (hip-*sip*-ill-ee) Queen of women of Lemnos who kill their husbands. Tries to get Jason to marry her.

Idas (*ee*-dass) Argonaut. Twin brother of Lynceus. Idas and Lynceus were from Sparta.

Idmon (*eed*-mon) Argonaut. A son of Apollo, killed by a wild boar.

Ino (*ee*-no) Daughter of Cadmus. Second wife of Athamas. Stepmother of Helle and Phrixus. She tries to trick Athamas into sacrificing his own children on Mount Laphystium. Kills herself when her plot is found out.

Jason (*jace*-on – real name **Diomedes** die-om-*ee*-deez). Captain of the Argonauts. Son of Aeson and Polymele. Brought up by Chiron in a cave on Mount Pelion. Vows to avenge his father, the rightful king of Iolcus, who has been deposed by Jason's step-uncle, Pelias. Pelias says Jason can have the throne of Iolcus if he brings back the Golden Fleece from Colchis. Jason has the *Argo* built, chooses 53 crew members and sets out.

King Laomedon of Troy (lau-*med*-on) King who vows to stop all Greek ships passing through the Hellespont after the Trojan War.

Lynceus (*lyn*-key-us) The *Argo*'s lookout. Twin brother of Idas and famed for his keen eyesight.

Medea (med-*dee*-a) Daughter of King Aites, sister of Chalciope and Apsyrtus, niece of Circe. Falls in love with Jason after Hera and Athene order Eros to fire a love arrow at her. Kills her brother Apsyrtus to help the Argonauts escape from Colchis with the Golden Fleece and hatches a plot to kill King Pelias. Also responsible for deaths of Princess Glaucis, King Creon and her own twin sons.

Melampus (*mell*-am-pus) Argonaut. A son of Poseidon. Can understand animals.

King Minos (*my*-noss) King of Crete and guardian of Talos, the robotic giant which attacks the *Argo* and is killed by Medea.

Mopsus (*mop*-sus) Argonaut. Can understand the language of birds.

Nauplius (*nor*-plee-us) The *Argo*'s navigator.

Nephele (*neff*-ee-lee) Demigoddess. Mother of Phrixus and Helle. A cloud-spirit: created from clouds by Zeus in the image of Hera.

Nymphs (*nimphs*) Demigoddesses, spirits of water, trees and mountains.

Oileus (*ee*-li-us) An Argonaut who is injured by the Symphalian birds.

Orpheus (*or*-fee-us) Argonaut. A singer and musician. The music of his magical lyre helps soothe the Dragon to sleep and drown out the Sirens' song.

King Pelias (*pee*-lee-ass) Half-brother of Jason's father, Aeson, and usurper of the throne of Iolcus. Vows to kill all Aeson's descendants. He sends Jason to get the Golden Fleece and kills Jason's baby brother, Promachus, in his absence. Killed by his own daughters, Evadne, Alcestis and Amphinome, who are tricked by Medea.

Periclymenus (perry-*klee*-men-us) Argonaut and shape-shifter. Son of Zeus. Can turn himself into anything he wants to be.

King Phineus (*fin*-ee-us) Blind King of Salmydessus who is plagued by the Harpies. The Argonauts drive the Harpies away and Phineus's advice helps them complete their quest.

Prince Phrixus (*fricks*-us) Son of Nephele and King Athamas. Stepson of Ino, brother of Helle. Travels to Colchis on the back of the golden ram. Marries Princess Chalciope and has four sons who are rescued by the Argonauts.

Pluto/Hades (*ploo*-toe/*hay*-deez) Brother of Zeus and king of the Underworld – the place where the Ancient Greeks believed people went after death.

Polydeuces (polly-*dyoo*-seez) (see **Castor**)

Polymele (polly-*mee*-lee) Jason's mother and wife of Aeson. Kills herself after her baby son, Promachus, is savagely killed by King Pelias.

Polyphemus (polly-*fee*-muss) Argonaut. A young rower.

Poseidon (poss-*eye*-don) Bad-tempered god of the sea. Controls storms, sea-monsters and earthquakes. Brother of Zeus.

Promachus (*pro*-mack-us) Jason's baby brother, killed by King Pelias.

Prometheus (prom-*ee*-thee-us) A Titan who stole fire from the gods and gave it to mankind. As a punishment he was chained to a rock and an eagle was sent to tear out his liver; the liver regrew every day and was torn out again and again.

Rhea (*ree*-a) A Titaness. Mother of Zeus, Poseidon and Pluto.

The Sirens (*sye*-runs) Monsters with the faces of beautiful women. Live on a rocky island and lure men to their doom with their singing. The Argonauts manage to sail safely past with the help of Orpheus and Hera. Only Butes succumbs.

The Stymphalian birds (stim-*fail*-ee-an birds) Birds with bronze beaks, feathers and claws. They attack the Argonauts near the Island of Ares, but are driven off by Atalanta and other archers.

Talos (*ta*-los) A huge, robotic bronze giant created by Hephaestus. Guardian of the Island of Crete, appointed by King Minos

Telamon (tell-*a*-mon) One of the Argonauts. An archer and rower.

Theseus (*thee*-syoos) Son of King Aegeus. Greek adventurer and hero.

Titan/Titaness (*tie*-tan/*tie*-tan-ess) One of the immortal race who were rulers of the world until the gods revolted and banished them.

Tiphys (*tee*-fiss) The pilot and helmsman who steers the *Argo*. He dies during the quest and is replaced by Ancaeus.

Ulysses (*yoo*-liss-eez) (also known as Odysseus) Hero of the Trojan War, King of Ithaca.

Zetes and Calais (*zee*-teeze and kall-*a*-iss) Argonauts. The winged sons of the North Wind, Boreas. They drive away the Harpies at King Phineus's palace.

Zeus (*zyoos*) King of the gods and father of the human race. Ruler of the sky. Married to his sister Hera. Rules from Mount Olympus and often gets involved in human affairs. All-powerful.

Important places

The Clashing Rocks (also known as **The Symplegades**) Two huge rocks which guarded the entrance to the Black Sea, at the mouth of the Bosphorus. They crashed together when ships tried to sail between them. Only the Argonauts got through.

Delphi (*dell*-fee) Site of the oracle, where priestesses foretold the future. People came from all over Greece to consult them.

Mount Olympus (oh-*limp*-us) The high mountain where the Ancient Greeks believed Zeus and the other gods and goddesses lived (except for Pluto and Poseidon who had their own kingdoms – the Underworld and the sea).

River Styx (*sticks*) River that dead people had to cross to enter the Underworld.

The Symplegades (sim-*pleg*-a-deez) see **Clashing Rocks**

The Underworld Underground kingdom ruled by Pluto. The Ancient Greeks believed all humans went when they died. Also called **Hades** (*hay*-deez).

First published in 1997 by Usborne Publishing Ltd, Usborne House, 83-85 Saffron Hill, London EC1 8RT, England. First published in America August 1997. Copyright © Usborne Publishing Ltd 1997. UE

Printed in Portugal